The Alden Family Mysteries
by Gertrude Chandler Warner

THE BOXCAR CHILDREN
SURPRISE ISLAND
THE YELLOW HOUSE MYSTERY
MYSTERY RANCH
MIKE'S MYSTERY
BLUE BAY MYSTERY
THE WOODSHED MYSTERY
THE LIGHTHOUSE MYSTERY
MOUNTAIN TOP MYSTERY
SCHOOLHOUSE MYSTERY
CABOOSE MYSTERY
HOUSEBOAT MYSTERY
SNOWBOUND MYSTERY
TREE HOUSE MYSTERY
BICYCLE MYSTERY
MYSTERY IN THE SAND
MYSTERY BEHIND THE WALL
BUS STATION MYSTERY
BENNY UNCOVERS A MYSTERY

The Boxcar

Children

by Gertrude Chandler Warner

Illustrated by
L. Kate Deal

ALBERT WHITMAN & Company, Niles, Illinois

ISBN 0-8075-0852-7

127 129 130 128 126

Printed in the U.S.A.

Table of Contents

The Boxcar Children

I—The Four Hungry Children

ONE WARM NIGHT four children stood in front of a bakery. No one knew them. No one knew where they had come from.

The baker's wife saw them first, as they stood looking in at the window of her store. The little boy was looking at the cakes, the big boy was looking at the loaves of bread, and the two girls were looking at the cookies.

Now the baker's wife did not like children. She did not like boys at all. So she came to the front of the bakery and listened, looking very cross.

"The cake is good, Jessie," the little boy said. He was about five years old.

"Yes, Benny," said the big girl. "But bread is better for you. Isn't it, Henry?"

"Oh, yes," said Henry. "We must have some bread, and cake is not good for Benny and Violet."

"I like bread best, anyway," said Violet. She was about ten years old, and she had pretty brown hair and brown eyes.

"That is just like you, Violet," said Henry, smiling at her. "Let's go into the bakery.

Maybe they will let us stay here for the night."

The baker's wife looked at them as they came in.

"I want three loaves of bread, please," said Jessie.

She smiled politely at the woman, but the woman did not smile. She looked at Henry as he put his hand in his pocket for the money. She looked cross, but she sold him the bread.

Jessie was looking around, too, and she saw a long red bench under each window of the bakery. The benches had flat red pillows on them.

"Will you let us stay here for the night?" Jessie asked. "We could sleep on those benches, and tomorrow we would help you wash the dishes and do things for you."

Now the woman liked this. She did not like to wash dishes very well. She would

like to have a big boy to help her with her
work.

"Where are your father and mother?" she
asked.

"They are dead," said Henry.

"We have a grandfather in Greenfield, but
we don't like him," said Benny.

Jessie put her hand over the little boy's
mouth before he could say more.

"Oh, Benny, keep still!" she said.

"Why don't you like your grandfather?"
asked the woman.

"He is our father's father, and he didn't
like our mother," said Henry. "So we don't
think he would like us. We are afraid he
would be mean to us."

"Did you ever see him?" asked the woman.

"No," answered Henry.

"Then why do you think he would be
mean to you?" asked the woman.

"Well, he never came to see us," said
Henry. "He doesn't like us at all."

"Where did you live before you came here?" asked the woman.

But not one of the four children would tell her.

"We'll get along all right," said Jessie. "We want to stay here for only one night."

"You may stay here tonight," said the woman at last. "And tomorrow we'll see what we can do."

Henry thanked her politely.

"We are all pretty tired and hungry," he said.

The children sat down on the floor. Henry cut one of the loaves of bread into four pieces with his knife, and the children began to eat.

"Delicious!" said Henry.

"Well, I never!" said the woman.

She went into the next room and shut the door.

"I'm glad she is gone," remarked Benny, eating. "She doesn't like us."

"Sh, Benny!" said Jessie. "She is good to
let us sleep here."

After supper the children lay down on
their red benches, and Violet and Benny
soon went to sleep.

But Jessie and Henry could hear the woman
talking to the baker.

She said, "I'll keep the three older children. They can help me. But the little boy
must go to the Children's Home. He is too
little. I cannot take care of him."

The baker answered, "Very well. Tomorrow I'll take the little boy to the Children's

Home. We'll keep the others for awhile, but we must make them tell us who their grandfather is."

Jessie and Henry waited until the baker and his wife had gone to bed. Then they sat up in the dark.

"Oh, Henry!" whispered Jessie. "Let's run away from here!"

"Yes, indeed," said Henry. "We'll never let Benny go to a Children's Home. Never, never! We must be far away by morning, or they will find us. But we must not leave any of our things here."

Jessie sat still, thinking.

"Our clothes and a cake of soap and towels are in the big laundry bag," she said. "Violet has her little workbag. And we have two loaves of bread left. Have you your knife and the money?"

"Yes," said Henry. "I have almost four dollars."

"You must carry Benny," said Jessie. "He will cry if we wake him up. But I'll wake Violet.

"Sh, Violet! Come! We are going to run away again. If we don't run away, the baker will take Benny to a Children's Home in the morning."

The little girl woke up at once. She sat up and rolled off the bench. She did not make any noise.

"What shall I do?" she whispered softly.

"Carry this," said Jessie. She gave her the workbag.

Jessie put the two loaves of bread into the laundry bag, and then she looked around the room.

"All right," she said to Henry. "Take Benny now."

Henry took Benny in his arms and carried him to the door of the bakery. Jessie took the laundry bag and opened the door very

softly. All the children went out quietly.
They did not say a word. Jessie shut the
door, and then they all listened. Everything
was very quiet. So the four children went
down the street.

II—Night Is Turned into Day

SOON THE CHILDREN left the town and came to a road. The big yellow moon was out, and they could see the road very well.

"We must walk fast," said Henry. "I hope the baker and his wife don't wake up and find us gone."

They walked down the road as fast as they could.

"How far can you carry Benny?" asked Violet.

"Oh, I can carry him a long way," replied Henry.

But Jessie said, "I think we could go faster if we woke him up now. We could take his hands and help him along."

Henry stopped and put Benny down.

"Come, Benny," he said. "You must wake up and walk now."

"Go away!" said Benny.

"Let me try," said Violet. "Now, Benny, you can play that you are a little brown bear and are running away to find a nice warm bed. Henry and Jessie will help you, and we'll find a bed."

Benny liked being a little brown bear, and so he woke up and opened his eyes. Henry and Jessie took his hands, and they all went on again.

They passed some farmhouses, but the houses were dark and quiet. The children did not see anyone. They walked and walked for a long time. Then the red sun began to come up.

"We must find a place to sleep," said Jessie. "I am so tired."

Little Benny was asleep, and Henry was carrying him again. The other children began to look for a place.

At last Violet said, "Look over there." She was pointing at a big haystack in a field near a farmhouse.

"A fine place, Violet," said Henry. "See what a big haystack it is!"

They ran across the field toward the farmhouse. They jumped over a brook, and then they came to the haystack. Henry was still carrying Benny.

Jessie began to make a nest in the haystack for Benny, and when they put him into it, he went to sleep again at once. The other children also made nests.

"Good night!" said Henry, laughing.

"It is 'Good morning,' I should think," replied Jessie. "We sleep in the day, and we walk all night. When it is night again, we'll wake up and walk some more."

The children were so tired that they went right to sleep. They slept all day, and it was night again when they woke up.

Benny said at once, "Oh, Jessie, I'm hungry. I want something to eat."

"Good old Benny," said Henry. "We'll have supper."

Jessie took out a loaf of bread and cut it into four pieces. It was soon gone.

"I want some water," begged Benny.

"Not now," said Henry. "You may have some water when it gets dark. There is a pump near the farmhouse. But if we leave the haystack now, someone will see us."

When it was dark, the children came out of the haystack and went quietly toward the farmhouse, which was dark and still. Nearby was a pump, and Henry pumped water as quietly as he could. He did not even wake up the hens and chickens.

"I want a cup," said Benny.

"No, Benny," whispered Henry. "You will have to put your mouth right in the water. You can play you are a horse."

This pleased Benny. Henry pumped and pumped, and at last Benny had all the water he wanted. The water was cold and sweet, and all the children drank. Then they ran across the field toward the road.

"If we hear anyone," said Jessie, "we must hide behind the bushes."

Just as she said this, the children heard a horse and cart coming up the road.

"Keep very still, Benny!" whispered Henry. "Don't say a word."

The children got behind the bushes as fast as they could, for they did not have much time to hide. The horse came nearer and

nearer and began to walk up the hill toward them. Then the children could hear a man talking. It was the baker!

"I wonder where those children went," he said. "I don't think they could walk as far as Silver City. If we don't find them in Greenfield, we'll go home."

"Yes," answered his wife. "I do not want to find them, anyway. I don't like children, but we must try a little while longer. We will look for them in Greenfield, and that's all."

The children watched until the horse and cart had gone down the road. Then they came out from behind the bushes and looked at each other.

"My, I am glad those people did not see us!" said Henry. "You were a good boy, Benny, to keep still.

"We'll not go to Greenfield."

"I wonder how far it is to Silver City," said Jessie.

The children were very happy as they walked along the road. They knew that the baker would not find them. They walked until two o'clock in the morning, and then they came to some signs by the side of the road.

The moon came out from behind the clouds, and Henry could read the signs.

"One sign says that Greenfield is this way," he said. "The other sign points to Silver City. We don't want to go to Greenfield. Let's take this other road to Silver City."

They walked for a long time, but they did not see anyone.

"Not many people come this way, I guess," said Henry. "But that is all the better."

"Listen!" said Benny suddenly. "I hear something."

"Listen!" said Violet.

The children stood still and listened, and they could hear water running.

"I want a drink of water, Henry!" said Benny.

"Well, let's go on," said Henry, "and see where the water is. I'd like a drink, too."

Soon the children saw a drinking fountain by the side of the road.

"Oh, what a fine fountain this is!" said Henry, running toward it. "See the place for people to drink up high, and a place in the middle for horses, and one for dogs down below."

All the children drank some cold water.

"Now I want to go to bed," said Benny.

Jessie laughed. "You can go to bed very soon."

Henry was looking down a little side road, which had grass growing in the middle of it.

"Come!" he cried. "This road goes into the woods. We can sleep in the woods."

"This is a good place," said Jessie, as they walked along. "It is far away from people. You can tell that by the grass in the road."

"And it will be near the drinking fountain," said Violet.

"That's right!" cried Henry. "You think of everything, Violet."

"It is almost morning," remarked Jessie. "And how hot it is!"

"I'm glad it is hot," said Henry, "for we must sleep on the ground. Let's find some pine needles for beds."

The children went into the woods and soon made four beds of pine needles.

"I hope it's not going to rain," said Jessie, as she lay down.

Then she looked up at the sky.

"It looks like rain, for the moon has gone behind the clouds."

She shut her eyes and did not open them again for a long time.

More clouds rolled across the sky, and the wind began to blow. There was lightning, also, and thunder, but the children did not hear it. They were all fast asleep.

III—A New Home in the Woods

AT LAST Jessie opened her eyes. It was
morning, but the sun was covered
by clouds. She sat up and looked
all around her, and then she looked at the

sky. It seemed like night, for it was very dark. Suddenly it began to thunder, and she saw that it was really going to rain.

"What shall we do? Where shall we go?" thought Jessie.

The wind was blowing more and more clouds across the sky, and the lightning was very near.

She walked a little way into the woods, looking for a place to go out of the rain.

"Where shall we go?" she thought again.

Then she saw something ahead of her in the woods. It was an old boxcar.

"What a good house that will be in the rain!" she thought.

She ran over to the boxcar. There was no engine, and the track was old and rusty. It was covered with grass and bushes because it had not been used for a long time.

"It *is* a boxcar," Jessie said. "We can get into it and stay until it stops raining."

She ran back as fast as she could to the other children. The sky was black, and the wind was blowing very hard.

"Hurry! Hurry!" cried Jessie. "I have found a good place! Hurry as fast as you can!"

Henry took Benny's hand, and they all ran through the woods after Jesssie.

"It's beginning to rain!" cried Henry.

"We'll soon be there," Jessie shouted back. "It is not far. When we get there, you must help me open the door. It is heavy."

The stump of a big tree stood under the door of the boxcar and was just right for a step. Jessie and Henry jumped up on the old dead stump and rolled back the heavy door of the car. Henry looked in.

"There is nothing in here," he said. "Come, Benny. We'll help you up."

Violet went in next, and, last of all, Jessie and Henry climbed in.

They were just in time. How the wind did blow! They rolled the door shut, and then it really began to rain. Oh, how it did rain! It just rained and rained. The children could hear it on the top of the boxcar, but no rain came in.

"What a good place this is!" said Violet. "It is just like a warm little house with one room."

After awhile the rain and lightning and thunder stopped, and the wind did not blow so hard. Then Henry opened the door and looked out. All the children looked out into the woods. The sun was shining, but some water still fell from the trees. In front of the boxcar a pretty little brook ran over the rocks, with a waterfall in it.

"What a beautiful place!" said Violet.

"Henry!" cried Jessie. "Let's live here!"

"Live here?" asked Henry.

"Yes! Why not?" said Jessie. "This box-

car is a fine little house. It is dry and warm
in the rain."

"We could wash in the brook," said Violet.

"Please, Henry," begged Jessie. "We could
have the nicest little home here, and we
could find some dishes, and make four beds
and a table, and maybe chairs!"

"No," said Benny. "I don't want to live
here, Jessie."

"Oh. dear, why not, Benny?" asked Jessie.

"I'm afraid the engine will come and take
us away," answered Benny.

Henry and Jessie laughed. "Oh, no,
Benny," said Henry. "The engine will never
take this car away. It is an old, old car, and
grass and bushes are growing all over the
track."

"Then doesn't the engine use this track
any more?" asked Benny.

"No, indeed," said Henry. He was beginning to want to live in the boxcar, too.

"We'll stay here today, anyway."

"Then can I have my dinner here?" asked Benny.

"Yes, you shall have dinner now," said Henry.

So Jessie took out the last loaf of bread and cut it into four pieces, but it was very dry. Benny ate the bread, but soon he began to cry.

"I want some milk, too, Jessie," he begged.

"He ought to have milk," said Henry. "I'll go to the next town and get some."

But Henry did not want to start. He looked to see how much money he had. Then he stood thinking.

At last he said, "I don't want to leave you girls alone."

"Oh," said Jessie, "we'll be all right, Henry. We'll have a surprise for you when you come back. You just wait and see!"

"Good-by, Henry," said Benny.

So Henry walked off through the woods.

When he had gone, Jessie said, "Now, children, what do you think we are going to do? What do you think I saw over in the woods? I saw some blueberries!"

"Oh, oh!" cried Benny. "I know what blueberries are. Can we have blueberries and milk, Jessie?"

"Yes," Jessie was beginning. But she suddenly stopped, for she heard a noise. Crack, crack, crack! Something was in the woods.

IV—Henry Has Two Surprises

JESSIE WHISPERED, "Keep still!"
The three children did not say a word. They sat quietly in the boxcar, looking at the bushes.

34

"I wonder if it's a bear," thought Benny.

Soon something came out. But it wasn't a bear. It was a dog, which hopped along on three legs, crying softly and holding up a front paw.

"It's all right," said Jessie. "It's only a dog, but I think he is hurt."

The dog looked up and saw the children, and then he wagged his tail.

"Poor dog," said Jessie. "Are you lost? Come over here and let me look at your paw."

The dog hopped over to the boxcar, and the children got out.

Jessie looked at the paw and said, "Oh, dear! You poor dog! There is a big thorn in your foot."

The dog stopped crying and looked at Jessie.

"Good dog," said Jessie. "I can help you, but maybe it will hurt."

The dog looked up at Jessie and wagged his tail again.

"Violet," ordered Jessie, "please wet my handkerchief in the brook."

Jessie sat down on the stump and took the dog in her lap. She patted him and gave him a little piece of bread. Then she began to pull out the thorn. It was a long thorn, but the dog did not make any noise. Jessie pulled and pulled, and at last the thorn came out.

Violet had a wet handkerchief ready. Jessie put it around the dog's paw, and he looked up at her and wagged his tail a little.

"He wants to say 'Thank you,' Jessie!" cried Violet. "He is a good dog not to cry."

"Yes, he is," agreed Jessie. "Now I had better hold him for awhile so that he will lie down and rest his leg."

"We can surprise Henry," remarked Benny. "Now we have a dog."

"So we can," said Jessie. "But that was not my surprise. I was going to get a lot of blueberries for supper."

"Can't we look for blueberries, while you hold the dog?" asked Violet.

"Yes, you can," said Jessie. "Look over there by the big trees."

Benny and Violet ran over to look.

"Oh, Jessie!" cried Benny. "Did you ever see so many blueberries? I guess five blueberries! No, I guess ten blueberries!"

Jessie laughed. "I guess there are more than five or ten, Benny," she said. "Get a clean towel and pick them into it."

For awhile Jessie watched Benny and Violet picking blueberries.

"Most of Benny's blueberries are going into his mouth," she thought with a laugh. "But maybe that's just as well. He won't get so hungry waiting for Henry to come back with the milk."

She carried the dog over to the children and sat down beside them, the dog on her lap. With her help the towel was soon full of blueberries.

"I wish we had some dishes," Jessie said. "Then we could have blueberries and milk."

"Never mind," said Violet. "When Henry comes, we can eat some blueberries and then take a drink of milk."

When Henry came, he had some heavy bundles. He had four bottles of milk in a bag, a loaf of brown bread, and also some fine yellow cheese.

He looked at the dog.

"Where did you get that fine dog?" he cried.

"He came to us," said Benny. "He is a surprise for you."

Henry went over to the dog, who wagged his tail. Henry patted him and said, "He ought to be a good watchdog. Why is the handkerchief on his foot?"

"He had a big thorn in his foot," answered Violet, "and Jessie took it out and put on the handkerchief. It hurt him, but he did not cry or growl."

"His name is Watch," remarked Benny.

"Oh, is it?" asked Jessie, laughing. "Watch is a good name for a watchdog."

"Did you bring some milk?" asked Benny, looking hungrily at the bottles.

"I should say I did!" replied Henry. "Four bottles!"

"Poor old Benny!" said Jessie. "We'll have dinner now. Or is it supper?"

"It must be supper," said Henry, "for soon we'll have to go to bed."

"Tomorrow we'll eat three times," said Jessie.

Now Jessie liked to have things in order, and so she put the laundry bag on some pine needles for a tablecloth. Then she cut the loaf of brown bread into five big pieces. The cheese was cut into four.

"Dogs don't like cheese," remarked Benny. The poor little boy was glad, too, for he was very hungry.

Violet put the four bottles of milk on the table, and Jessie put some blueberries and cheese at each place.

"Blueberries!" cried Henry. "Jessie, you had *two* surprises for me!"

"I'm sorry we haven't any cups," Jessie said. "We'll have to drink out of the bottles. Now all come and sit down."

So supper began. "Look, Benny," said

Henry. "You take some blueberries, then eat some brown bread, then some cheese, then take a drink of milk."

"It's good!" said Benny. He began to put more blueberries into his mouth.

The dog had supper, too. Jessie gave him bread as he lay on the ground beside her, and he drank milk out of her hand.

When supper was over, there was some milk left in each bottle.

"We'll have the rest of the milk for breakfast," said Jessie. "Tonight we are going to sleep on beds. Let's get some pine needles now."

Soon the children had a big pile. Henry jumped into the boxcar, and Jessie gave him the pine needles. He made four beds in one end of the car.

"This side is the bedroom," said Jessie.

"What will the other side be?" asked Benny.

"The other side?" asked Jessie. "Let me think. I guess that will be the sitting-room, and maybe some of the time it will be the kitchen."

Then she said, "Come, now. Come and get washed." She took the cake of soap and went down to the brook.

"That will be fun, Benny," said Violet. "We'll splash our 'paws' in the brook just as Little Brown Bear does." She knew that Benny did not like to be washed.

The children were all very hot, and so they were glad to splash in the cold water. Benny put cold water and soap on his face with the others and dried his hands on a towel.

"We'll have to have a line to dry the towels on," said Jessie.

So she took the string out of the laundry bag and tied one end of it to a tree. The other end of the string she tied to the boxcar. This made a good clothesline. When she had washed one towel and Violet had washed the other one, they hung both towels on the clothesline.

"It looks like home," said Henry. "See the washing!" He laughed.

Jessie was thinking.

"We ought to get some water to drink before we go to bed," she said. "But what shall we put it in?"

"Let's put all the milk into two bottles," said Henry. "Then we can fill the other two with water."

"Good," said Jessie. "You go alone to the fountain, Henry. You can hide if anyone comes along."

Henry went out very quietly, and soon came back with two bottles full of cold water. Benny drank a little, but he was almost asleep.

The other children helped him into the boxcar. Then they all climbed in, Jessie carrying the dog. He lay down at once beside her.

"It is so hot that we'll leave the door open," said Henry.

Soon they were fast asleep, dog and all. The moon came up, but they did not see it. This was the first time in four days that they could go to sleep at night, as children should.

V—The Explorers Find Treasure

THE NEXT MORNING Jessie woke up first, and she got up at once, for she was the housekeeper. The dog sat in the door of the car and looked at her as she jumped down to get the milk for breakfast. Then he jumped down after her.

Jessie walked down by the little brook and stopped to look at the waterfall. It was beautiful.

"I must look in the refrigerator," she said with a laugh.

It was a funny refrigerator. There was a rock behind the waterfall, and the night before Jessie had put the two bottles of milk in a hole in this rock. Now she took out the bottles and found that the milk was very cold.

"Is it good?" called Benny, who sat in the car door.

"It is delicious!" cried Jessie. "It is cold, too."

She got up into the car with the milk and sat down beside Benny. Then the four children drank the milk for breakfast.

Henry said, "Today I'll go to town and try

to get some work to do. I can cut grass or work in a garden or something. Then we'll have something besides milk for breakfast."

He washed his hands and face and started out.

"I'm so glad you have a dog, Jessie," he said. "Good-by! I'll be back at noon."

The children looked after Henry, and then they looked at Jessie.

"What are we going to do now, Jessie?" Benny asked his sister.

"Well, Benny," answered Jessie, "we'll go exploring and look for treasures. We'll begin here at the car and look and look until we find a dump."

"What's a dump?" asked Benny.

"Oh, Benny!" said Violet. "You know what a dump is. Old tin cans and old dishes and bottles."

"Are old tin cans and dishes treasures?" Benny wanted to know.

"They will be treasures for us," answered Jessie, laughing.

"And wheels?" asked Benny again. "Will there be any wheels on the dump?"

"Yes, maybe," replied Violet. "But cups, Benny, and plates, and maybe spoons. You like to drink milk out of a cup."

"Oh, yes," agreed Benny politely. But anyone could see that his mind was still on wheels.

The explorers started walking down the old rusty tracks, with Watch hopping along on three legs. The other paw, still tied up with Jessie's handkerchief, was held off the ground. But the dog looked very happy. He liked these kind children.

They all walked along through the woods, looking this way and that. After awhile the old track came out into the sun, and the explorers found that they were on top of a hill. They could look down and see the town below them.

"Henry is down there," said Jessie.

Benny was walking along behind his two sisters.

Suddenly he cried happily, "Look, Jessie! There's a treasure—a wheel!"

The girls looked where he was pointing, and they saw a big dump with many old bottles and tin cans on it. There were also both wheels and cups. Indeed, there were dishes of all kinds.

"Oh, Benny!" cried Jessie. "You saw the treasures first. What should we do without you!"

Violet ran over to the dump. "Here's a white pitcher, Jessie!" she cried.

Jessie looked at it. It was all right, with only one small crack.

"Here's a big white cup, too," she said, happily.

"Can you use a teapot, Jessie?" asked Benny.

"Yes, indeed!" she replied. "We can put water in it. I have found two cups and a bowl. Let's look for spoons, too!"

Violet held up what she had found—five spoons, covered with rust.

"Good!" said Jessie. "Here's a big kettle. Let's pile all the dishes in it. Then we can carry them back to the boxcar."

Benny had found four wheels just alike and laid them to one side. Now he held up a pink cup. There was a big crack in it, but it had a handle.

"This will be my pink cup," said Benny.

"I hope it will hold milk," said Jessie, laughing. "It's a beautiful cup, Benny."

The children laid all their treasures, even the wheels, on a board, and the girls carried the board back to the boxcar between them. They put the dishes down by the brook.

"Now we must wash them," said Jessie.

"All right," agreed Benny. "We'll wash my pink cup."

And never did a little boy hand dishes so carefully to his sisters as Benny did.

The girls washed the dishes with soap, and Jessie used sand to get the rust off the spoons.

"There!" she said, washing the last shining spoon. "How fine they look! But I'm afraid they still aren't clean enough to eat from. When Henry comes, we'll get him to build a fire. Then we can have hot water to rinse them, and they will be *very* clean."

The children sat back and admired the dishes.

Suddenly Violet cried, "Oh, I know where to put them. Come and see what I found in the car last night."

Both girls looked in at the door.

"Look on the door on the other side of the car," said Violet.

All Jessie saw were two pieces of wood nailed to the closed door of the car. But she knew at once what was in Violet's mind. She ran to get the board they had carried from the dump and laid it carefully across the two pieces of wood. It made a fine shelf for the dishes.

"There!" said Jessie.

The children could hardly wait to put the shining dishes on the shelf.

"Let's put them on now," said Violet, "and see how they look, without waiting to rinse them."

When they were on the shelf, Violet picked some white and yellow flowers and put them in a cup full of water in the middle of the shelf.

"There!" said Jessie, stepping back to look at it.

"You said 'There' three times," remarked Benny happily.

"So I did," replied Jessie, laughing. "And I'm going to say it again."

She pointed into the woods and said, "There!"

Henry was coming through the woods, and he carried many funny-looking bundles in his arms. But he would not open his bundles or tell what he had been doing until it was time for dinner.

"Where did you get the dishes?" he cried, when he saw the shelf.

"We went exploring," said Violet, "and found a big dump."

The children began telling him about their treasures. Benny told him about the tin cans and his pink cup and his wheels. Jessie took out the big kettle and asked him about building a fire.

"We want to use the dishes to eat from," she told him, "and it's hard to get them clean in cold water."

So Henry made a small fire in an open place where it could not burn anything. He put big stones all around it.

"We ought to have a fireplace," he remarked.

Jessie cleaned the kettle with sand and filled it with water. Then Henry put it on the fire. Soon the water was boiling, and Jessie rinsed the dishes carefully.

"Now I know they're clean enough to eat from," she said happily.

VI—A Queer Noise in the Night

AT LAST IT WAS dinner time, and the children sat down to see what Henry had in his bundles.

"I bought another loaf of brown bread at the store," said Henry, "and some more milk. Then I bought some dried meat, because we can eat it in our hands. And I bought a bone for Watch."

Watch looked hungrily at the bone and lay down at once to eat it.

Jessie got out four cups and bowls and put some milk into each one. Then the children put in little pieces of brown bread and began to eat it with their new spoons.

"What fun!" cried Jessie. "Eating with spoons. Now tell us what you did in town, Henry."

Henry began, "The town below this hill is Silver City. I saw the name on a sign.

"I went into the town and walked along the first street I came to. It was a nice street, with big houses and flowers and trees. I saw a man out cutting his grass. He's a good man, too, I can tell you—a doctor."

"Did you work for him?" asked Jessie.

"Yes," said Henry. "He was very hot, and just as I came to the house, his bell rang. He started to the house, and I called after him and asked him if I could cut the grass. He said, 'Yes, yes! I wish you would!' You see, he wasn't used to cutting it himself.

"So I cut the grass, and he said, 'Good for you. Do you want to work every day?' And he said he had never had a boy who cut it as well as I did."

"Oh, Henry!" cried Violet and Jessie.

"I told him I did want to work, and he told me to come back this afternoon.

"He has a pretty house and a garage and a big vegetable garden. Then he has a lot of cherry trees behind the house—a cherry orchard. You should see the beautiful big red cherries!

"Well, when I was cutting the grass near the kitchen, the cook came to the kitchen door and watched me.

"She asked me if I liked cookies. I said I did, and she gave me one."

"What did you do with it?" asked Benny hungrily.

"When she went back into the kitchen, I put it in my pocket," said Henry laughing."

"Did she see you?" cried Jessie.

"Oh, no," said Henry. "I played I was eating it. For a long time I carefully ate away on nothing at all."

Benny began to look at Henry's pocket. It did look very funny.

Henry went on. "When I came home, the doctor gave me a dollar, and the cook gave me this bag."

Henry laughed at Benny and pulled the bag out of his pocket. In it were ten delicious brown cookies.

"Oh, oh!" cried Benny. "Please, Jessie! Let's have cookies for dinner."

"Yes, indeed," said Jessie.

Then Henry opened his last bundle.

"I thought we ought to have a tablecloth," he said. "So I got one at the store. But it wasn't hemmed."

Violet begged, "Oh, let me hem it."

She took her scissors out of her workbag and cut the two ends even. But before she began to hem the pretty blue tablecloth, she helped Jessie wash and rinse the dishes and put them away. Benny helped, too. When Henry said good-by and went back to town, all the children were working happily.

Watch was trying to make a hole with one paw to bury his bone in.

"I'll help you bury your bone, Watch," said Benny.

"Oh, no, Benny," said Jessie. "Watch wants to bury his bone himself. You come and help me. I'm going to make a broom for the house."

For a little while Benny ran around finding sticks for the broom, but he soon went to sleep on the ground with the dog for a pillow.

The two girls sat by the brook. Violet was hemming the blue tablecloth, and Jessie was making the broom with a long stick for a handle.

When Henry came back at supper time, the broom with its long handle stood in the kitchen, and the new tablecloth was hemmed. Henry admired the broom and the tablecloth. Then he gave Jessie a small bundle.

"Oh, butter!" cried Jessie, her eyes shining.

It was butter, yellow and sweet. The four children had not had any butter for many days. At last they sat down to their fine supper.

"Now this spoon is a magic spoon," said Henry. "Turn it around and use the handle, and it is a knife!"

He showed Benny how to put the butter

on the brown bread with his magic knife. With dried meat, bread and butter, milk, and cookies, the children could not ask for a better supper.

"What did you do this afternoon, Henry?" asked Jessie.

"Well, I washed the doctor's car," said Henry. "Then I washed the walks and the windows. Tomorrow I'm going to work in the garden."

Then he looked at the brook. "Oh, how I would love to have a swim in that nice cold water!"

Henry was hot and sticky as he looked at the waterfall.

"Maybe we could make a swimming pool," he said. "We could build a dam out of logs."

"Oh, yes, we could," said Jessie. "Violet and I know where to find some logs and some big flat stones."

"You do?" said Henry.

"Yes," said Jessie. "They are not far away. And just a little way below here is a pool now, with sand all around it. But it is not big enough to swim in."

"Is that so!" cried Henry. "Some day I'll stay at home, and we'll try to dam up the brook and make a swimming pool."

"You can have my wheels," said Benny.

"Good!" replied Henry. "I'll make you a little cart with the wheels, Benny, and you can carry stones in it."

"Yes," said Benny. "I will."

"Come now, we must go to bed," said Jessie.

The children were all glad to go to bed. They stood on the stump and climbed into their new house, and they all went to sleep but Henry. He was thinking about the new swimming pool. All at once he saw that Watch was not asleep.

Henry patted the dog and said, "Lie down, Watch."

But Watch did not lie down. He began to growl softly.

"Sh!" said Henry to the dog. He sat up. Jessie sat up.

"What is it, Henry?" she whispered.

"I don't know," replied Henry. He was frightened.

"I think Watch hears something in the woods."

"Let's close the door," said Jessie. "I'm afraid."

The two children closed the heavy door softly. Then they sat still and listened, but they did not hear anything.

"Lie down, Watch," said Jessie again. "Go to sleep."

But Watch did not go to sleep. He growled again.

"Maybe someone is in the woods. Maybe

someone wants to hide in this car," whispered
Jessie.

"Maybe," said Henry. "There is something out there that the dog doesn't like."

Then they heard a stick crack, and Watch
barked.

"Oh, sh!" Jessie put her hand over his
mouth.

"If there is someone out in the woods, he
knows that there is a dog in this boxcar,"
said Henry.

He took the new broom in his hand and
waited.

But nothing came. Nothing at all. The two

children waited and waited. Violet and Benny slept through it all.

"I'm going to open the door now," said Henry.

They opened the door softly and then listened. The dog sniffed a little. Then he turned around three times and lay down. He put his head on his paws.

"It must be all right now," said Henry. "Watch knows. Maybe it was just a rabbit."

So at last they all went to sleep and slept until morning.

VII—A Big Meal from Little Onions

THE NEXT MORNING Jessie and Henry talked about the queer noise. They did not tell Violet and Benny.

"What do you think it was?" asked Jessie. "Do you think it was a rabbit?"

"I don't know," said Henry. "But I think someone was in the woods. I am glad we weren't hurt. Someone must have stepped on a stick and made it crack."

"What shall we do?" asked Jessie.

"Nothing," said Henry. "Watch is a good watchdog. He loves us now, and if anyone tried to hurt us, Watch would take care of us. He would do more than growl. But after this, we must not let Benny go into the woods alone."

"I'll keep Benny and Violet with me all the time," said Jessie.

"Good!" said Henry. "And keep Watch with you all the time, too.

"Good morning, Benny. Time to get up. Today you must build something for me out of stones."

"What is it?" asked Benny eagerly.

"I'm not going to tell you," said Henry, laughing.

"You build it just as Jessie tells you, and you will see."

Henry was so eager to begin work that he ran all the way to town. The doctor came to the door and smilingly looked him over from head to foot.

"My mother will tell you what to do to-day," the doctor said. "She wants you to work in her garden."

Mrs. Moore, the doctor's mother, had a sweet face and looked very kind.

"Good morning, Henry," she said. "Do you know how to thin out vegetables?"

"Oh, yes," said Henry. "I like to work in a vegetable garden."

"I haven't had much time to take care of my garden," Mrs. Moore said. "There! See that?"

She pulled out a carrot. It had to come

out, for it was much too near the other carrots.

"Yes, I see," said Henry.

He began to thin out the carrots. Mrs. Moore watched him as he pulled out some of the little carrots and put them in a pile. He left the other carrots to grow. Then he began on the turnips.

"You are a good worker," said Mrs. Moore. "I can see that." She smiled at Henry. "You may thin out all these vegetables."

Then she went into the house and left Henry alone. He worked all the morning. He thinned out the carrots, turnips, and little onions.

The mill bells rang at noon, but Henry did not hear them. He still worked on in the hot sun. Then he saw Mrs. Moore looking at him.

"You have worked long enough now," she said. "You may come again this afternoon."

"What shall I do with the vegetables I pulled up?" Henry asked.

"Oh, I don't want them," said Mrs. Moore. "Just leave them in a pile."

"Do you mind if I take them?" asked Henry.

"No, indeed. Do you have chickens?" Then, without waiting for an answer, she went right on, "You have done good work. Here is a dollar."

Henry said, "Thank you," and was glad he did not have to answer about the chickens.

When Mrs. Moore went into the house, he took some of the little carrots and turnips and onions. If he had looked up, he would have seen Mrs. Moore in the window watching him. But he did not look up. He was too eager to get to the store and order some meat.

When he arrived at the boxcar, Benny told him, "The building is done. I helped with it."

The "building" was a fireplace, made of flat stones.

"Benny did a lot of the work," said Jessie. "He carried stones and found wood for the fire."

The fireplace was a very good one. The children and Watch had made a hole at the foot of a big rock between two trees. Flat stones were laid on the floor of this hole and around the sides. More big stones were put up to keep out the wind.

Jessie had found a heavy wire in the dump and had put the big kettle on it and tied the ends of the wire to the two trees. The kettle hung over the fireplace, and the fire was laid. Beside the fireplace was a big wood-pile.

"Fine! Fine!" cried Henry. "You have done well. Now see what I have."

The girls were delighted with the meat and the little vegetables. With Henry's knife they cut the meat into little pieces. Then they filled the kettle with water from the fountain and put the meat into it, with a tin plate for a cover. Henry started the fire, and it burned well at once.

Jessie cut the tops off the vegetables and washed them in the brook.

"I'll put them in after the meat has cooked awhile," she said.

Soon the water began to boil, and the stew began to smell good. Watch sat down and looked at it. He sniffed hungrily at it and barked and barked.

The children sat around the fireplace, eating bread and milk. Now and then Jessie stirred the stew with a big spoon.

"It will make a good meal," said Henry. "Keep it boiling and do not leave it. When I come home tonight, I'll bring you some salt. And whatever you do, don't get on fire!"

Violet pointed to the pitcher and teapot that she had filled with water.

"That's to put on Benny or Watch if he should get on fire," she said.

Henry laughed and went happily on his way. He wished he could stay and smell the stew boiling, but he thought he ought to work. So he went back to Dr. Moore's house.

He was very happy when Dr. Moore said, "Do you want to clean up this garage?"

The garage was not in very good order. Dr. Moore laughed when he saw Henry look around for a broom.

"I must go out now," said Dr. Moore. "You just clean this place up."

Henry began at once. First he opened all the boxes. On the biggest box he painted the word TOOLS with a long-handled brush and a can of paint he had found. On another box he painted NAILS. Then he picked over the things and put the tools in the toolbox and the nails in the nail-box. This was fun for Henry, because he liked to get things in order.

Henry found a lot of nails that were bent and covered with rust. He put them in his pocket.

"I'll ask the doctor for these bent nails," he said to himself. "They are no good to him, but they are fine for me. I can use every old nail I get."

Then he washed the floor and washed his paint brush.

When Dr. Moore came home, he found Henry putting brushes, paint cans, and other things on the shelf.

"My, my, my!" he cried. He looked at the garage and laughed and laughed. He laughed until his mother came out to see what he was laughing at.

"Look, Mother!" he said. "Look at those tools. Look at the shelf. Look at my hammers.

One, two, three, four hammers. Your hammer, my hammer, and two other hammers. They were all lost. Can you use a hammer, Henry?"

"Yes, indeed I can!" cried Henry.

"Take one," said Dr. Moore. "You found them all."

"Oh, thank you!" said Henry. He showed the doctor the bent nails and was told that he could have those, too. He could hardly wait now to start home, because he was so eager to show Benny and his sisters his new hammer and nails.

"Tomorrow will be Sunday," said Dr. Moore. "Will you come again the next day?"

"Oh, yes," replied Henry, who had lost all track of the days.

"The cherries must be picked," said the doctor. He looked at Henry in a queer way. "We could use any number of cherry pickers if they were all as careful as you."

"Could you?" asked Henry eagerly. "Well, I'll come."

So the three said good-by, and Henry started for home. He had another dollar, a pocket full of old nails, a hammer, and the pile of vegetables that he had left at noon. On the way home he bought some salt.

When he arrived at the boxcar, he began to smell a delicious smell.

"Onions!" he shouted, running up to the kettle. "I do like the smell of onions."

"I like the turnips best," said Violet.

Jessie took off the cover carefully and stirred in the salt, and Henry sniffed the brown stew. It was boiling and boiling.

"A ladle, of all things!" cried Henry "Where did you get it?"

"I found a tin cup in the dump," said Jessie. "We used a long stick for a handle and tied it to the cup with a piece of wire. It makes a fine ladle."

She ladled out the stew into plates and bowls and put a spoon in each one.

"Oh, oh!" said Benny. "I am so hungry. I must eat my supper!"

The meat was well cooked, and the vegetables were delicious. Violet passed her plate for more turnips.

"I'd like some more onions," said Henry.

All the children ate until they could eat no more.

"That was the best meal I ever ate," said Jessie.

"Me, too," said Violet.

"I have time tonight to make Benny's cart," remarked Henry. "We'll want a cart."

"Will you make it with my wheels?" asked Benny.

"Yes, with your wheels," answered Henry. "But you must cart stones in it when I get it done."

"Yes," said Benny. "I will cart stones or rocks or anything."

"Tomorrow will be Sunday, and I can stay at home," Henry went on. "Do you think it's all right, Jessie, to build the dam for a swimming pool on Sunday?"

"Yes, I do," said Jessie. "We are making the swimming pool so that we can keep clean."

Henry began happily to hammer out the bent nails with his new hammer. Soon he had some good nails.

"You and I will go and find some boards, Benny," he said. "Come on."

Soon the boys came back with some boards from the dump. Henry sat down and began to make the cart. He could not see very well, because it was getting dark and there was no moon. But at last the cart was done, and he gave it to Benny.

"Thank you," said Benny, politely.

After his sisters had admired the cart, Benny pulled it around just for fun. Then Henry put it in the boxcar for the night.

Henry said to Jessie, "I hope we do not hear that queer noise tonight."

"I hope not, too," said Jessie. Then she laughed. "Look at Benny," she said. "He has gone to sleep with his hand on his cart."

Henry laughed, too, but he laughed at himself, because he was going to sleep with his new hammer under his pillow.

VIII—A Swimming Pool at Last

THE BOXCAR CHILDREN were so tired that they slept until ten o'clock Sunday morning.

When they woke up at last, they hurried through breakfast and went to work on the swimming pool.

"We'll make a dam across the brook," said Henry.

"Here is my cart," said Benny. "I'll cart stones and logs in it."

"Good for you," laughed Henry.

First the four children went down the brook to look at the pool Jessie had seen. The water was quiet here, and there was clean sand all around the little pool.

"It's big enough for a swimming pool," Henry remarked, "but I don't think it's deep enough."

He put a long stick in it to see how deep it was. When he looked at the wet stick, he found that the water was about a foot deep.

"The swimming pool should be three times as deep," he said. "Then it will be deep enough to swim in and won't be too deep for Benny. We'll build the dam here with logs and stones."

While the other children started the dam, Jessie washed all their stockings.

"We won't want our stockings on while we are working in the brook," she re-marked, as she rinsed them and hung them on the clothesline to dry. "So this is a good time to wash them."

It was hard work building the dam, but the children liked hard work. Henry and Jessie pulled the logs to the brook, and Violet and Benny carried the stones, with the help of the cart. Now and then Henry was called on to help with a heavy stone. But the two younger children carried most of them.

"Splash the stones right into the water," Henry told them. "But be careful to keep them in a line between these two trees."

The children watched with delighted eyes

as the wall of stones under the water began to grow higher and higher.

"The rock wall will help to hold the logs in place," said Henry.

At last it was time to lay the logs across the brook.

"Let's lay the first ones between these two trees," said Jessie. "Then the trees will hold both ends of the logs."

"Good work!" cried Henry, much pleased. "That's just what we'll do."

But when the first big log was splashed into place on top of the stone wall, the water began to run over the top of the log and around both ends.

"Oh, dear!" cried Jessie. "The water runs around the ends every time! What shall we do?"

"We'll have to put lots of logs on, with brush between them," said Henry. "We'll put on so many that the water *can't* get through."

They laid three logs across, with three more on top of them, and three more on top of those. Violet filled her arms with brush and held it in place until each log was laid. Benny filled the holes at the ends of the logs with flat stones. Such wet children never were seen before, but the hot sun would dry them off, and no one cared.

When the three top logs were laid in place at last, the four tired children sat down to watch the pool fill. But Henry could not sit still as the water came higher and higher up the dam.

"See how deep the pool is getting!" he cried. "See how still it is!"

At last the pool was full, and the water came over the top of the dam and made another waterfall.

"Just like a mill dam!" said Henry. "Now the pool is deep enough for all of us to swim in."

"You boys can have the first swim," said Jessie. "We girls must go and get dinner. We'll ring the bell when we are ready."

The boys splashed around in the pool, while the girls made a fire and hung the kettle of brown stew over it, stirring it now and then. Violet cut the bread and then got the butter, hard and cold, out of the refrigerator.

When everything was ready, Jessie rang the dinner bell. This bell was only a tin can from the dump. Jessie had hung it on a tree with a string, and she rang it with a spoon. Then she got the ladle and began ladling out the stew.

"That's the dinner bell," said Benny. "I know it is. Come, Watch. Don't you want some dinner?"

Watch had had a swim, too. He came out of the water and shook himself. The two boys put on their dry clothes and went to Sunday dinner.

"Let me ring the bell again," said Benny.

"I like stew even better today," said Henry, eating hungrily.

"That's because we worked so hard," remarked Jessie. "Let's go for a walk in the woods this afternoon."

"Oh, let's!" cried Violet. "Let's go exploring again."

The children washed the dishes and then started on their walk.

As they went along, Watch began to bark. At first the explorers were frightened.

"Oh, what is it?" cried Violet.

"Maybe it's a rabbit," said Henry.

Then they saw a hen running away

through the woods. Watch ran after her, but Henry called him back.

"Don't run after the poor hen," he said.

"The hen had a nest," remarked Benny.

"What?" asked Jessie.

"She had some eggs in it," said Benny. "Come here and see."

Jessie looked on the ground where Benny was pointing and saw a nest with five eggs in it.

"A runaway hen!" said Jessie. "She wanted to hide her nest so she would have some chickens. We'll have the eggs for supper. I know how to cook eggs."

The eggs made a delicious supper. Jessie put them in a bowl, with a little salt, and Violet took a spoon and stirred them as hard as she could.

"Put in some milk, Violet," said Jessie, "and stir them some more."

Henry started up the fire. The big kettle

was hung over the fire, and Jessie put in
some butter. She watched the butter until
it was nice and brown, and then she put in
the eggs.

"Sit down," she said. "Be all ready to eat
when the eggs are done."

Violet put the blue tablecloth on the
ground. She got the bread and butter and
the plates and spoons, and the children all
sat ready for supper.

"Here I come!" cried Jessie. "Hold out
your plates."

"Oh, Jessie!" cried Benny. "This is the
best meal I ever ate. I found the eggs, and
you cooked them."

"Yes, you did, Benny," said Henry. "Thank you for a fine meal."

"Tomorrow we'll have to eat bread and milk," said Jessie.

But when tomorrow came, the children had more than bread and milk, as you will soon see.

IX—Fun in the Cherry Orchard

THE NEXT MORNING Henry thought and thought about taking the other children to pick cherries with him.

At last he told his sisters about it as they ate bread and milk for breakfast.

"Dr. Moore said he wanted more children to help. Do you think all of us ought to go, Jessie?"

"Well," said Jessie, "I don't know. You see, there are four of us. If Grandfather is looking for us, it would be easier to see four than one."

"Yes, that's so," answered Henry. "But we can go down the hill and through the streets two by two. I'll take Benny and go ahead. Then in a little while you and Violet can come with the dog."

"Good!" said Jessie. "Watch can tell where you go."

The children took down the clothesline and shut the door of the car. Everything was in order. Then they started out.

When they arrived at the orchard, they soon saw that they were not the only workers. The doctor was there, and the cook, and two men carrying ladders and baskets.

"Good morning, Henry," said Mrs. Moore. "Can you work today?"

"Oh, yes," said Henry. "These are my sisters, Jessie and Violet. They can pick cherries, too. Benny is too young to climb trees, but we had to bring him."

"Maybe he can carry baskets," said Dr. Moore, smiling at Benny. "You see, this is a big cherry year, and we have to work fast, once we begin. Maybe he can help fill the little baskets from the big ones."

"Eat all you want," said Mrs. Moore. "The cherries are beautiful this year."

The children didn't eat all they wanted, but every now and then a big red cherry went into someone's mouth.

Henry and the girls went up the ladders and began to pick cherries. Watch barked for awhile. He did not like to have Jessie climbing the ladder. Then he sat down and looked at her up in the tree.

Benny hurried here and there, carrying baskets to the pickers and eating all the cherries he wanted. Everyone in the orchard liked Benny. The doctor laughed delightedly at him, and sweet Mrs. Moore fell in love with him at once. By and by he sat down beside her and carefully filled small baskets with cherries from the big baskets.

The men laughed at the funny things Benny said, and Watch barked happily. By and by the doctor left the orchard to make some calls.

At last Mrs. Moore said, "I never had such happy cherry pickers before. You are having such a good time out here that I don't want to go in the house." She smiled.

Mary, the cook, seemed to think the same thing, for she came again and again into the orchard.

After awhile the cook went in to get dinner, but the children still picked cherries. At noon Dr. Moore came home.

"You must stay to dinner," he said to the children. "We can eat here in the orchard under the trees. Will your mother be watching for you?" When he asked this, he looked at Henry in a queer way.

Henry did not know what to say. But at last Jessie said, "No. Our mother and father are dead."

"Then you must stay," said Mrs. Moore. "Here comes Mary."

The cook put a table under the trees, and they all sat around it and ate a delicious dinner. Then Mary went into the house and came out again with big bowls of cherry dumplings.

"I can smell something good!" cried Benny. "Is it cherries?"

"Yes, my little dear," said Mary. "Cherry

dumplings. The cherries are cooked in the dumplings."

Benny ate his cherry dumpling and then went to sleep with the dog for a pillow. But Henry and Jessie and Violet began to work again. Mrs. Moore looked out of the window at them.

"Just see how those children work," she said to Dr. Moore. "And they are so polite, too. I wonder who they are."

Dr. Moore said nothing. After awhile he went out to the orchard. "You have worked long enough," he said.

He gave them four dollars and all the cherries they could carry.

"That is too much," said Henry.

"No," said Dr. Moore, "it is just right. You see, you are better than most workers, because you are so happy. Come again."

"I'll come every day," said Benny.

They all laughed.

Dr. Moore saw that the children did not all leave the orchard at the same time, but started down the street two by two.

"I wish I knew who they are," he said to himself.

When the cherry pickers got back to their little home, they looked everything over carefully. But things were just as they had left them. The door was still closed, and the milk and butter were in the refrigerator. The children made a happy supper of bread and butter and cherries and then went to bed in the boxcar.

That same night Dr. Moore sat reading the paper. All at once he saw the word LOST and began to read.

"LOST. Four children, two boys and two girls. Somewhere around Greenfield or Silver City. Five thousand dollars to anyone who can find them.

James Henry Alden."

Dr. Moore sat up. "Five thousand dollars!" he said. "James Henry Alden! Oh, my! Oh, my!"

He sat still for a long time, thinking and laughing to himself.

"The four children are living in a boxcar, but I shall not tell Mr. Alden that they are his grandchildren," he said.

X—Henry and the Free-for-All

JAMES HENRY ALDEN was a very rich man.
His big mills stood just between Greenfield and Silver City.

Now J. H. Alden liked boys. He liked to see them running and jumping and playing. So each year, with three other rich men, he gave a Field Day to the town of Silver City. And even the mills were closed on Field Day.

Every year the boys were in training for the races. And not only boys, but men also, thin and fat, and girls trained for Field Day.

There were prizes for all kinds of races— running and swimming and jumping.

But the best one was a foot race, called a free-for-all, because anyone could run in it. Mr. Alden gave a prize of twenty-five dollars and a silver cup to the winner of the free-for-all. Sometimes a boy won the race, sometimes a girl. Once a fat man had won it.

On Field Day Henry was cutting the grass for Dr. Moore. Suddenly the doctor stopped his car in the street and called to Henry.

"Hop in," he said. "Today is Field Day, and I want you to see the races."

Henry hopped in, and the doctor started the car.

"I'm sorry I can't go," said Dr. Moore, "and I want to know all about it. I want you to tell me who wins each race."

Soon Henry found himself sitting on the bleachers. By and by a small boy climbed up the bleachers and sat beside him. Then a man called, "Free-for-all! Come and get ready!"

"What is that?" asked Henry. "A free-for-all?"

"Don't you know?" asked the small boy. "Didn't you see the one last year?"

"No," said Henry.

The boy laughed. "That was a funny one," he said. "There were two fat men in it, and some girls and boys. That boy over there won it. You should have seen him.

He ran so fast you could hardly see his legs at all!"

Henry looked at the winner of last year's race. He was smaller than Henry, but he was older. Suddenly Henry stood up and quietly left the bleachers. He went to the room where the boys were getting ready for the race.

"Do you want to run in the race?" a man asked him.

"Yes, I do," replied Henry.

The man gave him some track clothes to put on.

"Where did you train?" he asked.

"I never was trained," said Henry.

"These boys have been training all year," remarked the man.

"Oh, I don't think I'll win," answered Henry. "But I like to run. It's lots of fun, you know."

"So it is," said the man. "So it is."

Henry could hardly wait for the race to begin. He loved to run. But at last the race was called. It was time to start. Henry was Number 4.

Now Henry began to think. "It's a long race," he said to himself. "I must go easy at first."

The bell rang. Off went the runners down the track. In almost no time Henry was far behind most of the other runners. But he did not seem to mind this.

"It's fun to run, anyway," he said again to himself. And he tried to see how easily he could run.

All at once he had another thought. "I have tried to see how easily I can run," he said to himself. "Now I'll try to see how fast I can run."

Then all the people began to see how fast Henry could run. He ran faster and faster, and soon he passed the two girls ahead of

him. Then he passed a fat man and a little boy.

The people began to shout, "Number 4! Number 4!" Here was the kind of race they loved!

"Faster, faster!" cried Henry to himself. "I can run faster than this."

He could. He passed Number 25 and Number 6. Then he passed Number 5 and Number 10. Only one runner was ahead of Henry now. It was Number 16. Then Henry began to think of winning the race. He knew how much the twenty-five-dollar prize would mean to Jessie and the rest of the children.

"I am going to win this race!" he said to himself "I must pass Number 16."

He ran still faster. He could see the line at the end of the race.

"Number 4! Number 4!" shouted the people. "He is going to win!"

When Henry was near Number 16, he put his head down and ran as fast as he could. He passed Number 16 and went across the line! He had won!

The people shouted and shouted. Some men held Henry up high and carried him to Mr. Alden for the prize.

Then a man asked, "What is your name, boy?"

Henry did not know what to say. He did not want to tell his name. So he answered, "Henry James." Now this was Henry's name, but it was not all of his name.

At once the big sign said,

HENRY JAMES, NUMBER 4
WINNER OF FREE-FOR-ALL

"Here is the prize, Henry James," said Mr. Alden. "You can run well, my boy. I like to see you run."

He gave Henry a silver cup and the

twenty-five dollars. Then he shook hands with him.

Just then Dr. Moore came along and climbed up in the bleachers, but Henry did not see him. The doctor laughed to himself as Henry James shook hands with James Henry.

At last Henry got away from the people and started back to Dr. Moore's. He had the twenty-five-dollar prize in his pocket. When Dr. Moore came home and found Henry cutting the grass, he laughed quietly to himself.

"I just got home," said Henry. "I will tell you who won all the races."

Dr. Moore did not tell Henry that he had been up in the bleachers. He let Henry tell him about the races.

"And who won the free-for-all?" he asked.

"I did," said Henry.

"You did?" cried Dr. Moore. "Good for

you! What are you going to do with the money?"

"I'll give it to Jessie," answered Henry.

"Good," said the doctor again.

When Henry arrived at the boxcar with the twenty-five dollars, he found dinner ready. Jessie had boiled the rest of the vegetables and put butter on top. The children began to eat, but, hungry as they were, they stopped when Henry told them about the race and showed them the silver cup. They were so excited that they couldn't eat.

"You won the race, Henry?" cried Jessie, delighted. "Oh, I'm so glad!"

"You can run fast, Henry," said Benny. "I'm glad you won the race, too." He looked at the silver cup.

"I said my name was Henry James," said Henry.

"That's right," said Jessie. "So it is. You didn't have to change it."

"Are we rich now, Henry?" asked Benny.

"No, not very," said Henry, laughing. "By the way, I bought something for supper."

Jessie looked in the bag. There were some fat brown potatoes in it.

"Oh, I know how to cook these!" cried Jessie, happily. "They will be good. You just wait."

"I can't wait," said Henry, laughing. Then he went back to work.

After dinner, Benny played around with the dog.

"Benny," Jessie said suddenly, as she hung her dishtowels up to dry. "It's high time you learned to read."

"No," said Benny. "No school now."

Jessie laughed. "No," she said, "you can't go to school, but I can help you. I wish I had a book."

"We could make a book," said Violet. "We have all the papers left from bundles."

"So we could," replied Jessie. "But what could we use to make the words?"

"We could use a burned stick out of the fire," said Violet.

So Jessie put the end of a long stick into the fire and burned it black. Then she used the burned end to make words.

"Won't Henry be glad when he finds Benny can read?" cried Violet.

Now Benny did not want to learn to read. But he liked to watch the girls make the book. Jessie made the words SEE ME in the book. She called Benny. But he could not tell *see* from *me.*

"Don't you see, Benny?" said Jessie. "This one has an *s.* It says *see.* This one has *m.* It says *me.*"

But Benny did not see.

"It is too hard for me," he said.

"I'll tell you, Jessie," said Violet at last. "Let's make *see* on one paper and *me* on the other. That's the way they do in school. Then have him point to *see*."

The girls did this. They called Benny, and Jessie showed him again very carefully the word that said *see*. Then she put the two words down on the ground.

"Now, Benny, point to *see*," said Jessie.

Benny looked at the two words. He could not tell.

But Watch barked and put his paw on *see*.

Now Watch did not know one word from the other, but Benny thought he did. Was he going to let a dog get ahead of him? Not Benny! He looked at the words and learned them almost at once.

"Good old Watch!" said Jessie.

"It isn't hard at all," said Benny. "Is it, Watch?"

Before supper Benny could read,

"See me.

See me run.

I can run.

Can you run?"

"Good boy," said Jessie. "Now I must get supper."

The children started up the fire and washed the potatoes in the brook. Then Jessie put wet papers around them and put them in the fire under the hot stones.

"Are you going to burn them up, Jessie?" asked Benny.

"Oh, no, Benny," said Jessie. "You wait and see."

When Henry came home, he found Jessie rolling the potatoes out of the fire. They were very black.

"Oh, did you burn them up?" asked Henry.

"No, indeed," said Jessie. "Come and see." She gave three black potatoes to each one.

"They are very hot," said Violet. "Look out!"

"Open them," said Jessie, "and take out the potato with a spoon. Then put butter on top and some salt. I will get Benny's out. Well, how are they?"

"Oh!" cried Benny. "They are delicious!"

"What did I tell you?" said Jessie. "Have some milk!"

"Milk and potatoes make a very good supper," said Henry.

"I can read," remarked Benny.

"What!" said Henry.

"Yes, he can," said Violet. "He learned this afternoon. Go and get your book, Benny."

Benny liked to read now. "It is not hard," he said. "Watch can read, too."

"Oh, can he?" laughed Henry. "Let's see him."

"Watch is too tired now," said Benny. "I will read to you."

Benny read out of his new book.

"Good old Benny," said Henry. "Come to bed now. You must be tired with all that work, and I am tired, too."

XI—The Doctor Takes a Hand

THE DAYS WENT BY happily for the boxcar children. They found more treasures in the dump, and Henry worked every day for Dr. Moore.

One noon Henry came home with some new stockings for Benny. Benny was very happy about them and made everyone admire them. And when Jessie looked at the new stockings, she had a happy thought.

She carefully washed Benny's old stockings and hung them up to dry. That afternoon she and Violet sat down, with the workbag between them, to make a bear for Benny.

"You must make a tail, too, Jessie," begged Benny, watching her put on the arms and legs and head.

"Bears don't have tails," said Jessie. "Your old bear didn't have a tail."

"But this bear must have a tail," replied Benny, knowing that Jessie would put on two tails if he asked her to.

"What kind of tail?" asked Jessie at last.

"Long and thin," said Benny happily, "so I can pull it."

"Benny!" cried Jessie, laughing.

But she made a tail, long and thin, just as Benny had ordered.

"What's his name, Jessie?" asked Benny, when at last the bear was handed over to him.

"I haven't thought about a name," replied Jessie. "Why don't you think up a nice name for him?"

"Well, you made him out of my old stockings. Let's name him Stockings."

"All right, Stockings it is," agreed Jessie, trying not to laugh.

And from that day on, the bear's name was Stockings as long as he lived. And he lived to be a very old bear, indeed.

One afternoon Jessie saw how long Benny's hair was getting, and she cut it with Violet's scissors. Benny stood quietly while she did it.

But while his sisters were getting supper, he said to himself, "Jessie cut my hair. I'll get Violet's scissors and cut Watch's hair. He will look better."

He found Violet's scissors and made Watch lie down on his side. Then he began to cut the hair off.

Benny said, "Good dog, Watch. You are Jessie's dog, and so I will cut a J in your hair. Hold still now."

Watch lay still, and Benny began to cut a J. It was not a very good J, but it looked a little like one.

Soon Benny had cut off all the hair on one side, with a J in the middle. He stood admiring his work, and just then Jessie came to see what he was doing.

"Benny!" she cried. "What are you doing?" Then she began to laugh.

"Oh, Violet, come and see!" she called. "Watch looks so funny."

Jessie laughed and laughed until she almost cried. Violet laughed until she did cry.

Then she could not stop crying. She cried and cried. At last Jessie made up her mind that Violet was really sick.

"You must go to bed, Violet," she said. She helped her carefully into the boxcar and put pine needles all around her and under her. Then she wet a handkerchief in the cold water of the brook and laid it on her little sister's hot head.

"I wish Henry would come home!" said Jessie. "What shall we do?"

When Henry came at last, he looked at Violet and said that maybe she had a cold. "Maybe she sat too long by the brook," he said.

"If Violet is very sick, she ought to go to the hospital," said Jessie.

"Yes, I know that," said Henry. "And we don't want her to go to a hospital if we can help it. We should have to tell her name."

"Yes," said Jessie. "Then Grandfather could find us."

The two older children sat up with Violet. They put cold water on her head. But after dark Violet shook all over, and Jessie was frightened. She covered Violet all over with pine needles, but still she shook. They could not get her warm.

"I'm going to get Dr. Moore," said Henry. "I'm afraid Violet is very sick."

Then Henry started to run. He ran even faster than he had run in the race. Down the hill into the town he ran, until he came to Dr. Moore's house.

"Please come!" he cried. "Violet is very sick!"

The doctor said, "Come and get into my car."

He did not ask Henry which way to go, but the car went up the right road. When they came to the woods, he said to Henry, "Stay here in the car."

He ran alone up the hill to the boxcar. It seemed like magic that he knew where to go.

When Dr. Moore came back, he was carrying Violet in his arms. Jessie and Benny and Watch came, too. They all got into the car.

"Are you going to take her to a hospital?" asked Henry.

"No," said Dr. Moore. "I'm taking her to my house."

When they stopped at last, Dr. Moore car-

ried Violet into the house and said to his
mother, "Violet is very sick. We must put
her to bed."

Mrs. Moore hurried around, opening beds
and bringing pillows, and Mary came from
the kitchen with hot-water bottles. After
awhile Violet began to get warm.

Then Mrs. Moore came to get the other
children. "You must stay here all night,"
she said.

She gave Henry and Benny a big bed,
and Jessie slept in a little one. But Violet
was so sick that the doctor did not go to bed
all night. He would not leave her. He sat
by her side until ten o'clock in the morning.

Before ten o'clock a man came to see the
doctor. Mary told him he could wait. So he
sat down in the living-room. Soon Benny
came in.

"Where *is* the doctor?" asked the man,
crossly.

"He is up in Violet's room," answered Benny.

"This means five thousand dollars to him if he will come down," said the man.

"Oh, he can't come now," said Benny.

"What do you mean, boy?" asked the man. "What is he doing?"

"He's taking care of my sister Violet," said Benny. "She is sick."

"And you mean he wouldn't leave her even if I gave him five thousand dollars?" asked the man.

"Yes," answered Benny. "That's what I mean."

Then the man said, "You see, I have lost a little boy, and I think the doctor knows where he is. My little boy is just about as old as you are."

"Well, if you don't find him, maybe you can have me," remarked Benny. "I like you."

"You do?" cried the man. "Come and get up in my lap."

Benny climbed into the man's lap. "Have you got a dog?" he asked.

"No," said the man. "He is dead now. But you can see him in my watch. Here it is."

Benny looked at the dog. "He looks like a very good dog," he said. "I have a dog, too. His name is Watch."

Just then Watch came in with Dr. Moore.

"Good morning," said Dr. Moore. "Benny, you can go and play with Watch."

Benny ran out, and the man said, "Dr. Moore, where are my grandchildren?"

"That little boy is one of them," said Dr. Moore quietly.

"That beautiful little boy!" said the man.

"Yes," said Dr. Moore. "They are all good children. But they are afraid of you. They are afraid you will find them."

"How do you know that?" asked the man.

"They have changed their name," said the doctor. He looked at the man in a queer way. "The big boy changed his name on Field Day. You saw him then."

"I saw him? What did he change his name to?" asked the man.

"Henry James," said the doctor.

"The running boy!" cried the man. "The boy who won the free-for-all! I liked that boy. So I am his grandfather."

XII—James Henry and Henry James

D<small>R. MOORE WENT</small> to get his mother.
"Mother," he said, "this is Mr.
James Henry Alden. He wants to
take his grandchildren to live with him."

"I'm afraid they won't want to go with you," said Mrs. Moore, "until they learn to like you. And they won't want to go while Violet is so sick."

"Can't I see them?" begged Mr. Alden. "I won't tell them who I am."

"That would help," agreed the doctor. "If they grow to like you before they know who you are, things will be easier."

"Yes," said Mrs. Moore. "Stay here with us for awhile. The children will learn to like you, and then we can tell them that you are their grandfather."

"Thank you," said Mr. Alden. "I will go home and get some clothes and come back. And I will give you the five thousand dollars."

But Dr. Moore would not take the money.

"I just want these children to be happy," he said.

When Mary learned that she was to cook

for Mr. Alden, she was frightened. "How can I cook for him?" she cried. "He has everything. He is a very rich man."

"You can cook for anyone," said Dr. Moore, kindly. "Just get one of your good chicken dinners and make some cherry dumplings."

At dinner Mr. Alden saw all his grandchildren but Violet. He smiled with delight when he saw Jessie come into the room in her quiet way.

"Children," said Mrs. Moore, "this is Mr. Henry."

Benny laughed. "Henry and Mr. Henry," he remarked. "That is funny."

Henry shook hands with Mr. Alden before he sat down at the table.

"Where have I seen that man before?" he thought.

The children liked to hear Mr. Henry talk. He told them about a big cucumber in his garden. The cucumber was growing inside a bottle, and he couldn't get it out.

"Why not?" asked Benny.

"It is too big," said Mr. Alden.

"How did it get in?" asked Benny.

"It was a little cucumber when it went in," said Mr. Alden. "A cucumber will grow just the same in a bottle. It will grow so big you can't get it out."

"I'd like to see the cucumber," said Benny, stopping in the middle of his cherry dumpling.

"Would you really?" asked Mr. Alden, delighted. "Some day you and I will go over and pick it."

"And we can bring it to Violet," said Benny.

"Yes, we'll bring it to Violet," agreed Mr. Alden.

Henry thought again, "Where have I seen that man before? I wish I could remember."

He could not remember, but he liked Mr. Alden very much. All the children liked him because he was kind to them.

At last, one day, Mr. Alden could see Violet and went softly into her room with some beautiful flowers from his garden. The children loved him when he patted Violet's dark head and told her that he was sorry she had been sick.

He told her, too, about his garden, where the flowers came from.

"I'd like to see your garden," said Violet. "I love flowers."

"How long are you going to stay, Mr. Henry?" asked Benny.

"Sh, Benny!" said Jessie.

"I want to stay here as long as I can, my boy," said Mr. Alden quietly.

Henry looked at the man again. He knew that he had heard him say "my boy" before. Now where was it? He could not remember.

After dinner Mr. Alden sat under a tree, reading. Henry was working in the flower garden in front of the house. He looked at Mr. Alden again and again.

Suddenly it came to him, as the man smiled over his book. "It is the same man who gave me the twenty-five-dollar prize and the silver cup!" he said to himself. "I didn't remember him at first because I was so excited when he shook hands with me." He took another look and said again, "It's the very same man!"

Henry sat thinking for a little while. Then he got up and went to find Dr. Moore.

"Do you know who gave me the prize on

Field Day?" he asked the doctor. "Do you know what his name was?"

"James Alden, of the mills," replied the doctor. "J. H. Alden, over at Greenfield." He did not look at Henry while he was saying it.

Poor Henry was so surprised he almost fell over! That kind man his grandfather! He went out and sat on the steps to think it over.

To begin with, this man was too young. Henry had thought of his grandfather as being an old man with white hair. And Mrs. Moore had called him "Mr. Henry." Could it be that the man knew he was their grandfather and hadn't told them?

Then he saw that Mr. Alden was getting out of his chair under the trees.

"It's now or never," thought Henry. "I have to know!"

He walked eagerly after the man, who was

going toward the garden with his back to Henry. Then the man turned around and saw how excited Henry was.

"Are you James Henry Alden of Greenfield?" Henry asked.

"I am, my boy," replied Mr. Alden, with a smile. "Does that mean *you* know that *I* know you are Henry James Alden?"

"Yes," said Henry quietly.

Then James Henry Alden shook hands again with Henry James Alden.

Jessie and Benny came across the grass just in time to hear Henry say, "But, Grandfather—"

"Grandfather?" cried Jessie. "What do you mean, Henry?"

"Yes, Jessie," said Henry eagerly. "He's the man we have been running away from all this time."

"I thought you were old," said Benny "And cross. Jessie said so."

"I didn't know, Benny," said Jessie. Her face was red. To think of running away from this kind man!

But her grandfather did not seem to mind. He patted her on the head and said, "Let's go up and see Violet."

There was no stopping Benny. He hurried into Violet's room, holding Mr. Alden by the hand and shouting, "It's Grandfather, Violet! And he isn't cross after all!"

"What do you mean?" asked Violet. "Isn't he Mr. Henry?"

"My name is James Henry Alden," replied her grandfather.

"And my name is Henry James Alden," cried Henry.

"Well, well!" said Dr. Moore.

Violet held on to her grandfather's hand and listened to the rest talking excitedly.

"*Where* have you been living?" asked Mr. Alden at last.

They all looked at each other, even Dr. Moore and his mother. Then they all laughed as if they never would stop.

"You just ought to see!" said Dr. Moore.

"What!" cried all the children at once. "*You* never saw it in the daytime."

"Is that so?" laughed the doctor. "I have seen it many times in the daytime."

"Seen what?" asked Mr. Alden.

"Our house," said Jessie. "We have been living in a boxcar in the woods."

Then they all began to tell him about the dump and the dishes and the brook and the swimming pool.

"They have four beds of pine needles in the car," said Dr. Moore.

"How do you know?" asked Jessie.

"Well," said Dr. Moore, "the first day Henry worked for me, I walked after him as far as the hill."

"Why did you do that?" asked Mr. Alden.

"I liked him. I saw he was a fine boy, and I wanted to see where he lived."

"But you can't see the boxcar from the hill," said Jessie.

"No, but I came back that night and looked around," said Dr. Moore.

"About ten o'clock!" cried Jessie.

"Yes," said the doctor. "I stepped on a stick, and you heard me."

"Our rabbit!" cried Jessie and Henry. "Watch barked."

"Yes, I heard the dog bark. So I knew you were in the boxcar. Then I went home."

"But you came back?" asked Jessie.

"Oh, yes. When you were picking cherries, I went up to see your house. I wanted to see if you had enough to eat and enough dishes."

"Why didn't you tell me?" asked Mr. Alden. "Didn't you know they were my grandchildren?"

The doctor laughed. "Yes, I did. But they were having such a fine time that I didn't want to tell. They got along very well until Violet got sick. Then I told you."

"I'm glad you did," said Mr. Alden.

"I have seen your house, too," said Mrs. Moore. "I went up one day and saw all your dishes. I liked your big pitcher and teapot."

"All of you have seen it but me!" said Mr. Alden.

"We'll show it to you!" cried Benny. "I'll show you my cart made out of wheels, and my pink cup."

"Good for you, Benny," said his grandfather, much pleased. "When Violet gets

well, we'll all go up there. If you will show
me your house, I'll show you my house."

"Do you have a house?" asked Benny in
surprise.

"Yes. You can live there with me if you
like it. I have been looking for you children for a long time."

Violet was soon well again, and one afternoon they all started out to see the boxcar.
The doctor took them in his car. Many people looked out of their windows to watch Mr.
Alden and his grandchildren. They were
glad that the children had found such a kind
grandfather at last.

When they arrived at their old home, they
ran around, all talking excitedly. Watch
sniffed and sniffed all around, looking for
the bone he had buried. Everything was the
same.

"Here is the dam for the pool," said Henry
to his grandfather.

"See our 'building'!" shouted Benny, for that was what he called the fireplace. "It really burns, too. And this is the refrigerator in the waterfall, and here is my pink cup!"

They all stepped on the stump and climbed into the car. They looked at the four beds and the dishes.

"Here is the same old pitcher and teapot," said Jessie, laughing.

They found the blue tablecloth, and they all sat down by the brook and ate chicken and bread and butter and cookies. Benny drank milk from his pink cup.

"Come, we ought to go now," said Dr. Moore at last. "The sun is going down. I don't want Violet to take any more cold."

They closed the boxcar door and said good-by. But they were all sorry to go.

"Tomorrow," said Mr. Alden, "will all of you come to see my house?"

"Oh, yes," cried the children happily. They did not know what a beautiful house it was and what good times they were going to have in it.

XIII—A New Home for the Boxcar

THE CHILDREN'S grandfather wanted them to like his house. He wanted them to live with him all the time.

143

So he had made over some of the rooms just for them.

The children went with him in his car to see the house. When the car stopped in front of it, Henry cried in surprise, "Do you live *here*, in this beautiful house?"

It was a beautiful house. It was very big, with many trees and flower gardens around it.

"You may live here, too, if you like my house," remarked his grandfather, watching Henry's face.

The house was beautiful inside, too. There were flowers everywhere. There were maids everywhere. The children went up to the bedrooms.

"Oh!" cried Jessie. "This is Violet's room."

It really was Violet's room. There were violets on the wallpaper. The bed was white with a violet cover. On the table were flowers.

"What a beautiful room!" cried Violet, sitting down in a soft, pretty chair.

All the children shouted when they saw Benny's room. The wallpaper was blue and covered with big rabbits and dogs and bears. There were a rocking horse and a tool box and little tables and chairs. And an engine stood on a track, with cars almost as big as the little boy himself. Benny ran over to the engine.

"Can I run this train all day?" he asked. He sat down on the floor by the engine.

"Oh, no," said Henry. "You are going to school as soon as it begins."

His grandfather laughed. "That is right, my boy. You will like school. You will learn to read."

"Oh, I can read now," said Benny.

In Jessie's room they found a bed for Watch. It was on the floor by her bed. Watch got in at once, sniffed at the pillow, turned around three times, and lay down.

"He likes it," said Jessie. "He will sleep by me."

Just then the children heard a doorbell ring. A maid came up to find Mr. Alden.

"A man to see you," she said, "about the dog."

Now when Jessie heard the word *dog,* she was frightened. She was afraid it was about Watch.

"They won't take Watch away?" she whispered to Henry.

"No, indeed!" said Henry. "We'll never, *never* give him up."

Henry and Jessie and the other children went down with their grandfather to see the man, and Jessie was more frightened than ever. Watch did not growl at the man. He jumped up on him delightedly.

"You see, he was my dog," said the man. "But I sold him to a lady, and he ran away from her that very day. I have to turn him over to the lady I sold him to."

"How do you know he is the same dog?" asked Mr. Alden.

"Oh, he is my dog," said the man. "You see he knows me, and he has a small black spot on this foot. But someone has cut his hair on one side."

Benny looked. He found the black spot on Watch's foot.

"I never saw that spot before," said Henry.

"I will give you what you want for the dog," said Mr. Alden. "The children love him. They want to keep him."

"But I sold him to a lady," said the man. "I must take the dog to her."

Then Henry said, "Maybe she will want to change to another dog when she sees his hair. If she will agree to take another dog, will you let my grandfather have this one?"

"Yes, I will," said the man.

"Let's go and ask her, Grandfather," said Benny. "She will let Jessie have Watch. He is her dog. She took the thorn out of his foot."

The man told Mr. Alden where the lady lived, and they all started out to find her.

She was a very pretty young lady, and she asked them to sit down.

But Benny could not wait. He said, "Please let us keep Watch! I want him, and Jessie wants him, and we didn't know he was your dog."

"What do you mean?" asked the lady, laughing. "Who is Watch?"

"This dog is Watch," answered Henry. "A man came to Grandfather's house today and told us that he had sold the dog to you. When Watch ran away from you, the day you bought him, he came to us. He had a thorn in his foot, and Jessie took it out."

Watch looked up at the lady and wagged his tail. When she looked at him, she began to laugh.

"Look at his side!" she said. "Who cut his hair?"

"I'm sorry," said Henry. "Benny did that one day with Violet's scissors."

"I am not sorry," said the lady, laughing. "He looks so funny. And you want to keep him? Is that it?"

"Oh, yes," said Jessie eagerly. "The man will let us have him, if you will take another dog."

"Don't be afraid," said the young lady. "You may keep the dog. I can change to another one."

"Oh, thank you! You are nice!" cried Benny.

He ran to the lady and climbed up in her lap before anyone could stop him.

"I'd like to keep you, Benny, in place of the dog," laughed the lady, putting her arms around him.

How happy the children were to have Watch to keep! Mr. Alden gave the money to the man at once.

Four happy children sat with their grandfather around the Alden dinner table that night. The maids smiled in the kitchen to hear the children laugh. And the children laughed because Watch had a chair at the table beside Jessie and was really waited on by a maid.

Would you ever think that four children could be homesick in such a beautiful house? Jessie was the first one to wish for the old boxcar.

One day she said, "Oh, Grandfather, I'd like to cook something once more in the dear old kettle in the woods."

"Go out in the kitchen, my dear," said her grandfather. "The maids will help you. You can cook all you want to."

Jessie liked this, but it was not like the old days in the boxcar.

Then one day Benny said, "Grandfather, I wish I could drink my milk out of my dear old pink cup."

His grandfather began to think. He had

some pink cups, but they were not so dear to Benny as his old cracked one.

At last Mr. Alden said, "I am going to give you children a surprise."

"Is it very nice?" asked Benny.

"No, not very," laughed his grandfather. "It is not pretty at all."

"When will it come?" asked Benny.

"It will come today. You children must all go over to Dr. Moore's and stay, until the surprise comes."

"What can it be?" wondered Violet.

Her grandfather laughed. ' I hope you will like it," he said. "It is very heavy."

The children were glad to see sweet Mrs. Moore and the kind doctor again. They stayed until Mr. Alden said the surprise was ready. Then Dr. Moore and his mother went back with them in the big car.

Mr. Alden was as happy as a boy. He took them by the garage and through the big gar-

dens. At last they came to a garden with a
fountain in the middle and trees around it.
Near the fountain was the surprise. It was
the old boxcar!

The children ran over to it with cries of
delight, opened the door, and climbed in.
All the things were in place. Even the old
dead stump was there to step on.

Here was the old knife which had cut butter and bread and vegetables and firewood
and string. Here was Benny's pink cup, and
here was his bed. Here were the big kettle
and the blue tablecloth. Here were the
pitcher and the old teapot. And here was the
dinner bell which the children had made
from an old tin can.

Benny hung it on a tree with a string and
rang it over and over again with a spoon.
Watch rolled on the floor of the car and
barked and barked. Then he began to sniff
at everything.

"He's looking for the bone he buried," laughed Benny.

"How they love the old boxcar!" said Mrs. Moore. "I like to see them so happy."

"Thank you for the surprise, Grandfather," said Violet. "We'll never go away from you again."

"I hope not, my dear," said Mr. Alden. "We'll all live happily ever after."

And so they did.

GERTRUDE CHANDLER WARNER discovered when she was teaching that many readers who like an exciting story could find no books that were both easy and fun to read. She decided to try to meet this need, and her first book, *The Boxcar Children*, quickly proved she had succeeded.

Miss Warner drew on her own experiences to write the mystery. As a child she spent hours watching trains go by on the tracks opposite her family home. She often dreamed about what it would be like to set up housekeeping in a caboose or freight car—the situation the Alden children find themselves in.

When Miss Warner received requests for more adventures involving Henry, Jessie, Violet, and Benny Alden, she began additional stories. In each, she chose a special setting and introduced unusual or eccentric characters who liked the unpredictable.

While the mystery element is central to each of Miss Warner's books, she never thought of them as strictly juvenile mysteries. She liked to stress the Aldens' independence and resourcefulness and their solid New England devotion to using up and making do. The Aldens go about most of their adventures with as little adult supervision as possible—something else that delights young readers.

Miss Warner lived in Putnam, Connecticut, until her death in 1979. During her lifetime, she received hundreds of letters from girls and boys telling her how much they liked her books. And so she continued the Aldens' adventures, writing a total of nineteen books in the Boxcar Children series.

From the
Mixed-up Files of
Mrs. Basil E. Frankweiler

From the
Mixed-up Files of
Mrs. Basil E. Frankweiler

WRITTEN AND ILLUSTRATED BY

E. L. KONIGSBURG

A YEARLING BOOK

Published by
Bantam Doubleday Dell Books for Young Readers
a division of
Bantam Doubleday Dell Publishing Group, Inc.
1540 Broadway
New York, New York 10036

The trademarks Yearling® and Dell® are registered in the U.S. Patent and Trademark Office and in other countries.

ISBN: 0-440-43180-8

Reprinted by arrangement with Atheneum Publishers.
Printed in the United States of America
November 1977

61 60 59 58 57 56 55 54 53 52

OPM

To David, with love and pluses

From the
Mixed-up Files of
Mrs. Basil E. Frankweiler

To my lawyer, Saxonberg:

I can't say that I enjoyed your last visit. It was obvious that you had too much on your mind to pay any attention to what I was trying to say. Perhaps, if you had some interest in this world besides law, taxes, and your grandchildren, you could almost be a fascinating person. Almost. That last visit was the worst bore. I won't risk another dull visit for a while, so I'm having Sheldon, my chauffeur, deliver this account to your home. I've written it to explain certain changes I want made in my last will and testament. You'll understand those changes (and a lot of other things) much better after reading it. I'm sending you a carbon copy; I'll keep the original in my files. I don't come in until much later, but never mind. You'll find enough to interest you until I do.

You never knew that I could write this well, did you? Of course, you don't actually know yet, but you soon will. I've spent a lot of time on this file. I listened. I investigated, and I fitted all the pieces together like a jigsaw puzzle. It leaves no doubts. Well, Saxonberg, read and discover.

Mrs. Basil E. Frankweiler

1

CLAUDIA KNEW THAT SHE COULD NEVER PULL OFF the old-fashioned kind of running away. That is, running away in the heat of anger with a knapsack on her back. She didn't like discomfort; even picnics were untidy and inconvenient: all those insects and the sun melting the icing on the cupcakes. Therefore, she decided that her leaving home would not be just running from somewhere but would be running to somewhere. To a large place, a comfortable place, an indoor place, and preferably a beautiful place. And that's why she decided upon the Metropolitan Museum of Art in New York City.

She planned very carefully; she saved her allowance and she chose her companion. She chose Jamie, the second youngest of her three younger brothers. He could be counted on to be quiet, and now and then he was good for a laugh. Besides, he was rich; unlike most boys his age, he had never even begun collecting baseball cards. He saved almost every penny he got.

But Claudia waited to tell Jamie that she had decided upon him. She couldn't count on him to be *that* quiet for *that* long. And she calculated needing *that* long to save her weekly allowances. It seemed senseless to run away without money. Living in the suburbs had taught her that everything costs.

She had to save enough for train fare and a few expenses before she could tell Jamie or make final plans. In the meantime she almost forgot why she was running away. But not entirely. Claudia knew that it had to do with injustice. She was the oldest child and the only girl and was subject to a lot of injustice. Perhaps it was because she had to both empty the dishwasher and set the table on the same night while her brothers got out of everything. And, perhaps, there was another reason more clear to me than to Claudia. A reason that had to do with the sameness of each and every week. She was bored with simply being straight-A's Claudia Kincaid. She was tired of arguing about whose turn it was to choose the Sunday night seven-thirty television show, of injustice, and of the monotony of everything.

The fact that her allowance was so small that it took her more than three weeks of skipping hot fudge sundaes to save enough for train fare was another example of injustice. (Since you always drive to the city, Saxonberg, you probably don't know the cost of train fare. I'll tell you. Full fare one way costs one dollar and sixty cents. Claudia and Jamie could each travel for half of that since she was one month under twelve, and Jamie was well under twelve—being only nine.) Since she intended to return home after everyone had learned a lesson in Claudia appreciation, she had to save money for her return trip, too, which was like full fare one way. Claudia knew that hundreds of people who lived in her town worked in offices in New York City and could afford to pay full fare both ways every day. Like her father. After all, Greenwich was considered an actual suburb of New York, a commuting suburb.

Even though Claudia knew that New York City was not far away, certainly not far enough to go considering the size and number of the injustices done to her, she knew that it was a good place to get lost. Her mother's Mah-Jong club ladies called it *the city*. Most of them never ventured there; it was exhausting, and it made them nervous. When she was in the fourth grade, her class had gone on a trip to visit historical places in Manhattan. Johnathan Richter's mother hadn't let him go for fear he'd get separated from the group in all the jostling that goes on in New York. Mrs. Richter, who was something of a character, had said that she was certain that he would "come home lost." And she considered the air very bad for him to breathe.

Claudia loved the city because it was elegant; it was important; and busy. The best place in the world to hide. She studied maps and the Tourguide book of the American Automobile Association and reviewed every field trip her class had ever taken. She made a specialized geography course for herself. There were even some pamphlets about the museum around the house, which she quietly researched.

Claudia also decided that she must get accustomed to giving up things. Learning to do without hot fudge sundaes was good practice for her. She made do with the Good Humor bars her mother always kept in their freezer. Normally, Claudia's hot fudge expenses were forty cents per week. Before her decision to run away, deciding what to do with the ten cents left over from her allowance had been the biggest adventure she had had each week. Sometimes she didn't even have ten cents, for she lost a nickel every time she broke one of the household rules like forgetting to make her bed in the morning. She was certain that her allowance was the smallest in her class. And most of the other sixth graders never lost part of their pay since they had full-time maids to do the chores instead of a cleaning lady only twice a week. Once after she had started saving, the drug store had a special. HOT FUDGE, 27¢, the sign in the window said. She bought one. It would postpone her running away only twenty-seven cents worth. Besides, once she made up her mind to go, she enjoyed the planning almost as much as she enjoyed spending money. Planning long and well was one of her special talents.

Jamie, the chosen brother, didn't even care for hot fudge sundaes although he could have bought one at least every other week. A year and a half before, Jamie had made a big purchase; he had spent his birthday money and part of his Christmas money on a transistor radio, made in Japan, purchased from Woolworth's. Occasionally, he bought a battery for it. They would probably need the radio; that made another good reason for choosing Jamie.

On Saturdays Claudia emptied the wastebaskets, a task she despised. There were so many of them. Everyone in her family had his own bedroom and wastebasket except her mother and father who shared both—with each other. Almost every Saturday Steve emptied his pencil sharpener into his. She knew he made his basket messy on purpose.

One Saturday as she was carrying the basket from her parent's room, she jiggled it a little so that the contents would sift down and not spill out as she walked. Their basket was always so full since there were two of them using it. She managed to shift a shallow layer of Kleenex, which her mother had used for blotting lipstick, and thus exposed the corner of a red ticket. Using the tips of her forefinger and thumb like a pair of forceps, she pulled at it and discovered a ten ride pass for the New York, New Haven, and

Hartford Railroad. Used train passes normally do not appear in suburban wastebaskets; they appear in the pockets of train conductors. Nine rides on a pass are marked off in little squares along the bottom edge, and they are punched one at a time as they are used; for the tenth ride the conductor collects the pass. Their cleaning lady who had come on Friday must have thought that the pass was all used up since rides one through nine were already punched. The cleaning lady never went to New York, and Claudia's dad never kept close track of his pocket change or his train passes.

Both she and Jamie could travel on the leftover pass since two half fares equal one whole. Now they could board the train without having to purchase tickets. They would avoid the station master and any stupid questions he might ask. What a find! From a litter of lipstick kisses, Claudia had plucked a free ride. She regarded it as an invitation. They would leave on Wednesday.

On Monday afternoon Claudia told Jamie at the school bus stop that she wanted him to sit with her because she had something important to tell him. Usually, the four Kincaid children neither waited for each other nor walked together, except for Kevin who was somebody's charge each week. School had begun on the Wednesday after Labor Day. Therefore, their "fiscal week" as Claudia chose to call it began always on Wednesday. Kevin was only six and in the first grade and was made much over by everyone, especially by Mrs. Kincaid, Claudia thought. Claudia also thought that he was terribly babied and impossibly spoiled. You would think that her parents would know something about raising children by the time Kevin, their fourth, came along. But her parents hadn't learned. She couldn't remember being anyone's charge when she was in the first grade. Her mother had simply met her at the bus stop every day.

Jamie wanted to sit with his buddy, Bruce. They played cards on the bus; each day meant a continuation of the day before. (The game was nothing very complicated, Saxonberg. Nothing terribly refined. They played *war*, that simple game where each player puts down a card, and the higher card takes both. If the cards are the same, there is a war which involves putting down more cards; winner then takes all the war cards.) Every night when Bruce got off at his stop, he'd take his stack of cards home with him. Jamie would do the same. They always took a vow not to shuffle. At the stop before Bruce's house, they would stop playing, wrap a rubber band around each pile, hold the stack under each other's chin and spit on each other's deck saying, "Thou shalt not shuffle." Then each tapped his deck and put it in his pocket.

Claudia found the whole procedure disgusting, so she suffered no feelings of guilt when she pulled Jamie away from his precious game. Jamie was mad, though. He was in no mood to listen to Claudia. He sat

slumped in his seat with his lips pooched out and his eyebrows pulled down on top of his eyes. He looked like a miniature, clean-shaven Neanderthal man. Claudia didn't say anything. She waited for him to cool off.

Jamie spoke first, "Gosh, Claude, why don't you pick on Steve?"

Claudia answered, "I thought, Jamie, that you'd see that it's obvious I don't want Steve."

"Well," Jamie pleaded, "want him! Want him!"

Claudia had planned her speech. "I want you, Jamie, for the greatest adventure in our lives."

Jamie muttered, "Well, I wouldn't mind if you'd pick on someone else."

Claudia looked out the window and didn't answer. Jamie said, "As long as you've got me here, tell me."

Claudia still said nothing and still looked out the window. Jamie became impatient. "I said that as long as you've got me here, you may as well tell me."

Claudia remained silent. Jamie erupted, "What's the matter with you, Claude? First you bust up my card game, then you don't tell me. It's undecent."

"Break up, not bust up. Indecent, not undecent," Claudia corrected.

"Oh, boloney! You know what I mean. Now tell me," he demanded.

"I've picked you to accompany me on the greatest adventure of our mutual lives," Claudia repeated.

"You said that." He clenched his teeth. "Now tell me."

"I've decided to run away from home, and I've chosen you to accompany me."

"Why pick on me? Why not pick on Steve?" he asked.

Claudia sighed, "I don't want Steve. Steve is one of the things in my life that I'm running away from. I want you."

Despite himself, Jamie felt flattered. (Flattery is as important a machine as the lever, isn't it, Saxonberg? Give it a proper place to rest, and it can move the world.) It moved Jamie. He stopped thinking, "Why pick on me?" and started thinking, "I am chosen." He sat up in his seat, unzipped his jacket, put one foot up on the seat, placed his hands over his bent knee and said out of the corner of his mouth, "O.K., Claude, when do we bust out of here? And how?"

Claudia stifled the urge to correct his grammar again. "On Wednesday. Here's the plan. Listen carefully."

Jamie squinted his eyes and said, "Make it complicated, Claude. I like complications."

Claudia laughed. "It's got to be simple to work. We'll go on Wednesday because Wednesday is music lesson day. I'm taking my violin out of its case and am packing it full of clothes. You do the same with your trumpet case. Take as much clean underwear as possible and socks and at least one other shirt with you."

"All in a trumpet case? I should have taken up the bass fiddle."

"You can use some of the room in my case. Also use your book bag. Take your transistor radio."

"Can I wear sneakers?" Jamie asked.

Claudia answered, "Of course. Wearing shoes all the time is one of the tyrannies you'll escape by coming with me."

Jamie smiled, and Claudia knew that now was the correct time to ask. She almost managed to sound casual. "And bring all your money." She cleared her throat. "By the way, how much money do you have?"

Jamie put his foot back down on the floor, looked out the window and said, "Why do you want to know?"

"For goodness' sake, Jamie, if we're in this together, then we're together. I've got to know. How much do you have?"

"Can I trust you not to talk?" he asked.

Claudia was getting mad. "Did I ask you if I could trust you not to talk?" She clamped her mouth shut and let out twin whiffs of air through her nostrils; had she done it any harder or any louder, it would have been called a snort.

"Well, you see, Claude," Jamie whispered, "I have quite a lot of money."

Claudia thought that old Jamie would end up

being a business tycoon someday. Or at least a tax attorney like their grandfather. She said nothing to Jamie.

Jamie continued, "Claude, don't tell Mom or Dad, but I gamble. I play those card games with Bruce for money. Every Friday we count our cards, and he pays me. Two cents for every card I have more than he has and five cents for every ace. And I always have more cards than he has and at least one more ace."

Claudia lost all patience. "Tell me how much you have! Four dollars? Five? How much?"

Jamie nuzzled himself further into the corner of the bus seat and sang, "Twenty-four dollars and forty-three cents." Claudia gasped, and Jamie, enjoying her reaction, added, "Hang around until Friday and I'll make it twenty-five even."

"How can you do that? Your allowance is only twenty-five cents. Twenty-four forty-three plus twenty-five cents makes only twenty-four dollars and sixty-eight cents." Details never escaped Claudia.

"I'll win the rest from Bruce."

"C'mon now, James, how can you know on Monday that you'll win on Friday?"

"I just know that I will," he answered.

"How do you know?"

"I'll never tell." He looked straight at Claudia to see her reaction. She looked puzzled. He smiled, and so did she, for she then felt more certain than ever that she had chosen the correct brother for a partner in escape. They complemented each other perfectly. She was cautious (about everything but money) and poor; he was adventurous (about everything but money) and rich. More than twenty-four dollars. That would be quite a nice boodle to put in their knapsacks if they were using knapsacks instead of instrument cases. She already had four dollars and eighteen cents. They would escape in comfort.

Jamie waited while she thought. "Well? What do you say? Want to wait until Friday?"

Claudia hesitated only a minute more before deciding, "No, we have to go on Wednesday. I'll write you full details of my plan. You must show the plan to no one. Memorize all the details; then destroy my note."

"Do I have to eat it?" Jamie asked.

"Tearing it up and putting it in the trash would be much simpler. No one in our family but me ever goes through the trash. And I only do if it is not sloppy and not full of pencil sharpener shavings. Or ashes."

"I'll eat it. I like complications," Jamie said.

"You must also like wood pulp," Claudia said. "That's what paper is made of, you know."

"I know. I know," Jamie answered. They spoke no more until they got off the bus at their stop. Steve got off the bus after Jamie and Claudia.

Steve yelled, "Claude! Claude! It's your turn to take Kevin. I'll tell Mom if you forget."

Claudia who had been walking up ahead with Jamie stopped short, ran back, grabbed Kevin's hand and started retracing her steps, pulling him along to the side and slightly behind.

"I wanna walk with Stevie," Kevin cried.

"That would be just fine with me, Kevin Brat," Claudia answered. "But today you happen to be my responsibility."

"Whose 'sponsibility am I next?" he asked.

"Wednesday starts Steve's turn," Claudia answered.

"I wish it could be Steve's turn every week," Kevin whined.

"You just may get your wish."

Kevin never realized then or ever that he had been given a clue, and he pouted all the way home.

2

On Tuesday night Jamie found his list of instructions under his pillow pinned to his pajamas. His first instruction was to forget his homework; get ready for the trip instead. I wholeheartedly admire Claudia's thoroughness. Her concern for delicate details is as well developed as mine. Her note to Jamie even included a suggestion for hiding his trumpet when he took it out of its case. He was to roll it up in his extra blanket, which was always placed at the foot of his bed.

After he had followed all the instructions on the list, Jamie took a big glass of water from the bathroom and sat cross-legged on the bed. He bit off a large corner of the list. The paper tasted like the bubble gum he had once saved and chewed for five days; it was just as tasteless and only slightly harder. Since the ink was not waterproof, it turned his teeth blue. He tried only one more bite before he tore up the note, crumpled the pieces, and threw them into the trash. Then he brushed his teeth.

The next morning Claudia and Jamie boarded the school bus as usual, according to plan. They sat together in the back and continued sitting there when they arrived at school and everyone got out of the bus. No one was supposed to notice this, and no one did. There was so much jostling and searching for homework papers and mittens that no one paid any attention to anything except personal possessions until they were well up the walk to school. Claudia had instructed Jamie to pull his feet up and crouch his head down so that Herbert, the driver, couldn't see him. He did, and she did the same. If they were spotted, the plan was to go to school and fake out their schedules as best they could, having neither books in their bags nor musical instruments in their cases.

They lay over their book bags and over the trumpet and violin cases. Each held his breath for a long time, and each resisted at least four temptations to peek up and see what was going on. Claudia pretended that she was blind and had to depend upon her senses of hearing, touch, and smell. When they heard the last of the feet going down the steps and the motor start again, they lifted their chins slightly and smiled—at each other.

Herbert would now take the bus to the lot on the Boston Post Road where the school buses parked. Then he would get out of the bus and get into his car and go wherever else he always went. James and Claudia practiced silence all during the ragged ride to the parking lot. The bus bounced along like an empty cracker box on wheels—almost empty. Fortunately, the bumps made it noisy. Otherwise, Claudia would have worried for fear the driver could hear her heart, for it sounded to her like their electric percolator brewing the morning's coffee. She didn't like keeping her head down so long. Perspiration was causing her cheek to stick to the plastic seat; she was convinced that she would develop a medium-serious skin disease within five minutes after she got off the bus.

The bus came to a stop. They heard the door open. Just a few backward steps by Herbert, and they would be discovered. They held their breath until they heard him walk down the steps and out of the bus. Then they heard the door close. After he got out, Herbert reached in from the small side window to operate the lever that closed the door.

Claudia slowly pulled her arm in front of her and glanced at her watch. She would give Herbert seven minutes before she would lift her head. When the time was up, both of them knew that they could get up, but both wanted to see if they could hold out a little bit longer, and they did. They stayed crouched down for about forty-five more seconds, but being cramped and uncomfortable, it seemed like forty-five more minutes.

When they got up, both were grinning. They peeked out of the window of the bus, and saw that the coast was clear. There was no need to hurry so they slowly made their way up to the front, Claudia leading. The door lever was left of the driver's seat, and as she walked toward it, she heard an awful racket behind her.

"Jamie," she whispered, "what's all that racket?"

Jamie stopped, and so did the noise. "What racket?" he demanded.

"You," she said. "You are the racket. What in the world are you wearing? Chain mail?"

"I'm just wearing my usual. Starting from the bottom, I have B.V.D. briefs, size ten, one tee shirt . . ."

"Oh, for goodness' sake, I know all that. What are you wearing that makes so much noise?"

"Twenty-four dollars and forty-three cents."

Claudia saw then that his pockets were so heavy they were pulling his pants down. There was a gap of an inch and a half between the bottom hem of his shirt and the top of his pants. A line of winter white skin was punctuated by his navel.

"How come all your money is in change? It rattles."

"Bruce pays off in pennies and nickels. What did you expect him to pay me in? Traveler's checks?"

"O.K. O.K.," Claudia said. "What's that hanging from your belt?"

"My compass. Got it for my birthday last year."

"Why did you bother bringing that? You're carrying enough weight around already."

"You need a compass to find your way in the woods. Out of the woods, too. Everyone uses a compass for that."

"What woods?" Claudia asked.

"The woods we'll be hiding out in," Jamie answered.

"Hiding *out in*? What kind of language is that?"

"English language. That's what kind."

"Who ever told you that we were going to hide out in the woods?" Claudia demanded.

"There! You said it. You said it!" Jamie shrieked.

"Said what? I never said we're going to hide out in the woods." Now Claudia was yelling, too.

"No! you said '*hide out in*.'"

"I did not!"

Jamie exploded. "You did, too. You said, 'Who ever told you that we're going to *hide out in* the woods?' You said that."

"O.K. O.K." Claudia replied. She was trying hard to remain calm, for she knew that a group leader must never lose control of herself, even if the group she leads consists of only herself and one brother brat.

"O.K.," she repeated. "I *may* have said hide *out in*, but I didn't say *the woods*."

"Yes, sir. You said, 'Who ever told you that . . .' "

Claudia didn't give him a chance to finish. "I know. I know. Now, let's begin by my saying that we are going to hide out in the Metropolitan Museum of Art in New York City."

Jamie said, "See! See! you said it again."

"I did not! I said, 'The Metropolitan Museum of Art.' "

"You said *hide out in* again."

"All right. Let's forget the English language lessons. We are going to the Metropolitan Museum of Art in Manhattan."

For the first time, the meaning instead of the grammar of what Claudia had said penetrated.

"The Metropolitan Museum of Art! Boloney!" he exclaimed. "What kind of crazy idea is that?"

Claudia now felt that she had control of herself and Jamie and the situation. For the past few minutes they had forgotten that they were stowaways on the school bus and had behaved as they always did at home. She said, "Let's get off this bus and on the train, and I'll tell you about it."

Once again James Kincaid felt cheated. "The train! Can't we even hitchhike to New York?"

"Hitchhike? and take a chance of getting kidnapped or robbed? Or we could even get mugged," Claudia replied.

"Robbed? Why are you worried about that? It's mostly my money," Jamie told her.

"We're in this together. Its mostly your money we're using, but it's all my idea we're using. We'll take the train."

"Of all the sissy ways to run away and of all the sissy places to run away to. . . ." Jamie mumbled.

He didn't mumble quite softly enough. Claudia turned on him, "Run *away to*? How can you run *away* and *to*? What kind of language is that?" Claudia asked.

"The American language," Jamie answered. "American James Kincaidian language." And they both left the bus forgetting caution and remembering only their quarrel.

They were not discovered.

On the way to the train station Claudia mailed two letters.

"What were those?" Jamie asked.

"One was a note to Mom and Dad to tell them that we are leaving home and not to call the FBI. They'll get it tomorrow or the day after."

"And the other?"

"The other was two box tops from corn flakes. They send you twenty-five cents if you mail them two box tops with stars on the tops. For milk money, it said."

"You should have sent that in before. We could use twenty-five cents more."

"We just finished eating the second box of corn flakes this morning," Claudia informed him.

They arrived at the Greenwich station in time to catch the 10:42 local. The train was not filled with either commuters or lady shoppers, so Claudia walked up the aisles of one car and then another until she found a pair of chairs that dissatisfied her the least with regard to the amount of dust and lint on the blue velvet mohair covers. Jamie spent seven of the twenty-eight-and-a-half railroad miles trying to convince his sister that they should try hiding in Central Park. Claudia appointed him treasurer; he would not only hold all the money, he would also keep track of it and pass judgment on all expenditures. Then Jamie began to feel that the Metropolitan offered several advantages and would provide adventure enough.

And in the course of those miles Claudia stopped regretting bringing Jamie along. In fact when they emerged from the train at Grand Central into the underworld of cement and steel that leads to the terminal, Claudia felt that having Jamie there was important. (Ah, how well I know those feelings of hot and hollow that come from that dimly lit concrete ramp.) And his money and radio were not the only reasons. Manhattan called for the courage of at least two Kincaids.

3

As soon as they reached the sidewalk, Jamie made his first decision as treasurer. "We'll walk from here to the museum."

"Walk?" Claudia asked. "Do you realize that it is over forty blocks from here?"

"Well, how much does the bus cost?"

"The bus!" Claudia exclaimed. "Who said anything about taking a bus? I want to take a taxi."

"Claudia," Jamie said, "you are quietly out of your mind. How can you even think of a taxi? We have no more allowance. No more income. You can't be extravagant any longer. It's not my money we're spending. It's *our* money. We're in this together, remember?"

"You're right," Claudia answered. "A taxi is expensive. The bus is cheaper. It's only twenty cents each. We'll take the bus."

"*Only* twenty cents each. That's forty cents total. No bus. We'll walk."

"We'll wear out forty cents worth of shoe leather," Claudia mumbled. "You're sure we have to walk?"

"Positive," Jamie answered. "Which way do we go?"

"Sure you won't change your mind?" The look on Jamie's face gave her the answer. She sighed. No wonder Jamie had more than twenty-four dollars; he was a gambler and a cheapskate. If that's the way he wants to be, she thought, I'll never again ask him for bus fare; I'll suffer and never, never let him know about it. But he'll regret it when I simply collapse from exhaustion. I'll collapse quietly.

"We'd better walk up Madison Avenue," she told her brother. "I'll see too many ways to spend *our* precious money if we walk on Fifth Avenue. All those gorgeous stores."

She and Jamie did not walk exactly side by side. Her violin case kept bumping him, and he began to walk a few steps ahead of her. As Claudia's pace slowed down from what she was sure was an accumulation of carbon dioxide in her system (she had not yet learned about muscle fatigue in science class even though she was in the sixth grade honors class), Jamie's pace quickened. Soon he was walking a block and a half ahead of her. They would meet when a red light held him up. At one of these mutual stops Claudia instructed Jamie to wait for her on the corner of Madison Avenue and 80th Street, for there they would turn left to Fifth Avenue.

She found Jamie standing on that corner, probably one of the most civilized street corners in the whole world, consulting a compass and announcing that when they turned left, they would be heading "due northwest." Claudia was tired and cold at the tips; her fingers, her toes, her nose were all cold while the rest of her was perspiring under the weight of her winter clothes. She never liked feeling either very hot or very cold, and she hated feeling both at the same time. "Head due northwest. Head due northwest," she mimicked. "Can't you simply say turn right or turn left as everyone else does? Who do you think you are? Daniel Boone? I'll bet no one's used a compass in Manhattan since Henry Hudson."

Jamie didn't answer. He briskly rounded the corner of 80th Street and made his hand into a sun visor as he peered down the street. Claudia needed an argument. Her internal heat, the heat of anger, was cooking that accumulated carbon dioxide. It would soon explode out of her if she didn't give it some vent. "Don't you realize that we must try to be inconspicuous?" she demanded of her brother.

"What's inconspicuous?"

"Un-noticeable."

Jamie looked all around. "I think you're brilliant, Claude. New York is a great place to hide out. No one notices no one."

"Anyone," Claudia corrected. She looked at Jamie and found him smiling. She softened. She had to agree with her brother. She was brilliant. New York was a great place, and being called brilliant had cooled her down. The bubbles dissolved. By the time they reached the museum, she no longer needed an argument.

As they entered the main door on Fifth Avenue, the guard clicked off two numbers on his people counter. Guards always count the people going into the museum, but they don't count them going out. (My chauffeur, Sheldon, has a friend named Morris who is a guard at the Metropolitan. I've kept Sheldon busy getting information from Morris. It's not hard to do since Morris loves to talk about his work. He'll tell about anything except security. Ask him a question he won't or can't answer, and he says, "I'm not at liberty to tell. Security.")

By the time Claudia and Jamie reached their destination, it was one o'clock, and the museum was busy. On any ordinary Wednesday over 26,000 people come. They spread out over the twenty acres of floor space; they roam from room to room to room to room to room. On Wednesday come the gentle old ladies who are using the time before the Broadway matinee begins. They walk around in pairs. You can tell they are a set because they wear matching pairs of orthopedic shoes, the kind that lace on the side. Tourists visit the museum on Wednesdays. You can tell them because the men carry cameras, and the women look as if their feet hurt; they wear high heeled shoes. (I always say that those who wear 'em deserve 'em.) And there are art students. Any day of the week. They also walk around in pairs. You can tell that they are a set because they carry matching black sketchbooks.

(You've missed all this, Saxonberg. Shame on you! You've never set your well-polished shoe inside that museum. More than a quarter of a million people come to that museum every week. They come from Mankato, Kansas where they have no museums and from Paris, France, where they have lots. And they all enter free of charge because that's what the museum is: great and large and wonderful and free to all. And complicated. Complicated enough even for Jamie Kincaid.)

No one thought it strange that a boy and a girl, each carrying a book bag and an instrument case and who would normally be in school, were visiting a museum. After all, about a thousand school children visit the museum every day. The guard at the entrance merely stopped them and told them to check their cases and book bags. A museum rule: no bags, food, or umbrellas. None that the guards can see. Rule or no rule, Claudia decided it was a good idea. A big sign in the checking room said NO TIPPING, so she knew that Jamie couldn't object. Jamie did object, however; he pulled his sister aside and asked her how she expected him to change into his pajamas. His pajamas, he explained, were rolled into a tiny ball in his trumpet case.

Claudia told him that she fully expected to check out at 4:30. They would then leave the museum by the front door and within five minutes would re-enter from the back, through the door that leads from the parking lot to the Children's Museum. After all, didn't that solve all their problems? (1) They would be seen leaving the museum. (2) They would be free of their baggage while they scouted around for a place to spend the night. And (3) it was free.

Claudia checked her coat as well as her packages. Jamie was condemned to walking around in his ski jacket. When the jacket was on and zippered, it covered up that exposed strip of skin. Besides, the orlon plush lining did a great deal to muffle his twenty-four-dollar rattle. Claudia would never have permitted herself to become so overheated, but Jamie liked perspiration, a little bit of dirt, and complications.

Right now, however, he wanted lunch. Claudia wished to eat in the restaurant on the main floor, but Jamie wished to eat in the snack bar downstairs; he thought it would be less glamorous, but cheaper, and as chancellor of the exchequer, as holder of the veto power, and as tightwad of the year, he got his wish. Claudia didn't really mind too much when she saw the snack bar. It was plain but clean.

James was dismayed at the prices. They had $28.61 when they went into the cafeteria, and only $27.11 when they came out still feeling hungry. "Claudia," he demanded, "did you know food would cost so much? Now, aren't you glad that we didn't take a bus?"

Claudia was no such thing. She was not glad that they hadn't taken a bus. She was merely furious that her parents, and Jamie's too, had been so stingy that she had been away from home for less than one whole day and was already worried about survival money. She chose not to answer Jamie. Jamie didn't notice; he was completely wrapped up in problems of finance.

"Do you think I could get one of the guards to play me a game of war?" he asked.

"That's ridiculous," Claudia said.

"Why? I brought my cards along. A whole deck."

Claudia said, "*Inconspicuous* is exactly the opposite of that. Even a guard at the Metropolitan who sees thousands of people every day would remember a boy who played him a game of cards."

Jamie's pride was involved. "I cheated Bruce through all second grade and through all third grade so far, and he still isn't wise."

"Jamie! Is that how you knew you'd win?"

Jamie bowed his head and answered, "Well, yeah.

Besides, Brucie has trouble keeping straight the jacks, queens, and kings. He gets mixed up."

"Why do you cheat your best friend?"

"I sure don't know. I guess I like complications."

"Well, quit worrying about money now. Worry about where we're going to hide while they're locking up this place."

They took a map from the information stand; for free. Claudia selected where they would hide during that dangerous time immediately after the museum was closed to the public and before all the guards and helpers left. She decided that she would go to the ladies' room, and Jamie would go to the men's room just before the museum closed. "Go to the one near the restaurant on the main floor," she told Jamie.

"I'm not spending a night in a men's room. All that tile. It's cold. And, besides, men's rooms make noises sound louder. And I rattle enough now."

Claudia explained to Jamie that he was to enter a booth in the men's room. "And then stand on it," she continued.

"Stand on it? Stand on what?" Jamie demanded.

"You know," Claudia insisted. "Stand on it!"

"You mean stand on the toilet?" Jamie needed everything spelled out.

"Well, what else would I mean? What else is there in a booth in the men's room? And keep your head down. And keep the door to the booth very slightly open," Claudia finished.

"Feet up. Head down. Door open. Why?"

"Because I'm certain that when they check the ladies' room and the men's room, they peek under the door and check only to see if there are feet. We must stay there until we're sure all the people and guards have gone home."

"How about the night watchman?" Jamie asked.

Claudia displayed a lot more confidence than she really felt. "Oh! there'll be a night watchman, I'm sure. But he mostly walks around the roof trying to keep people from breaking in. We'll already be in. They call what he walks, a cat walk. We'll learn his habits soon enough. They must mostly use burglar alarms in the inside. We'll just never touch a window, a door, or a valuable painting. Now, let's find a place to spend the night."

They wandered back to the rooms of fine French and English furniture. It was here Claudia knew for sure that she had chosen the most elegant place in the world to hide. She wanted to sit on the lounge chair that had been made for Marie Antoinette or at least sit at her writing table. But signs everywhere said not to step on the platform. And some of the chairs had silken ropes strung across the arms to keep you from even trying to sit down. She would have to wait until after lights out to be Marie Antoinette.

At last she found a bed that she considered perfectly wonderful, and she told Jamie that they would spend the night there. The bed had a tall canopy,

supported by an ornately carved headboard at one end and by two gigantic posts at the other. (I'm familiar with that bed, Saxonberg. It is as enormous and fussy as mine. And it dates from the sixteenth century like mine. I once considered donating my bed to the museum, but Mr. Untermyer gave them this one first. I was somewhat relieved when he did. Now I can enjoy my bed without feeling guilty because the museum doesn't have one. Besides, I'm not that fond of donating things.)

Claudia had always known that she was meant for such fine things. Jamie, on the other hand, thought that running away from home to sleep in just another bed was really no challenge at all. He, James, would rather sleep on the bathroom floor, after all. Claudia then pulled him around to the foot of the bed and told him to read what the card said.

Jamie read, "Please do not step on the platform."

Claudia knew that he was being difficult on purpose; therefore, she read for him, "State bed—scene of the alleged murder of Amy Robsart, first wife of Lord Robert Dudley, later Earl of . . ."

Jamie couldn't control his smile. He said, "You know, Claude, for a sister and a fussbudget, you're not too bad."

Claudia replied, "You know, Jamie, for a brother and a cheapskate, you're not too bad."

Something happened at precisely that moment.

Both Claudia and Jamie tried to explain to me about it, but they couldn't quite. I know what happened, though I never told them. Having words and explanations for everything is too modern. I especially wouldn't tell Claudia. She has too many explanations already.

What happened was: they became a team, a family of two. There had been times before they ran away when they had acted like a team, but those were very different from *feeling* like a team. Becoming a team didn't mean the end of their arguments. But it did mean that the arguments became a part of the adventure, became discussions not threats. To an outsider the arguments would appear to be the same because feeling like part of a team is something that happens invisibly. You might call it *caring*. You could even call it *love*. And it is very rarely, indeed, that it happens to two people at the same time—especially a brother and a sister who had always spent more time with activities than they had with each other.

They followed their plan: checked out of the museum and re-entered through a back door. When the guard at that entrance told them to check their instrument cases, Claudia told him that they were just passing through on their way to meet their mother. The guard let them go, knowing that if they went very far, some other guard would stop them again. However, they managed to avoid other guards for the

remaining minutes until the bell rang. The bell meant
that the museum was closing in five minutes. They
then entered the booths of the rest rooms.

They waited in the booths until five-thirty, when
they felt certain that everyone had gone. Then they
came out and met. Five-thirty in winter is dark, but
nowhere seems as dark as the Metropolitan Museum
of Art. The ceilings are so high that they fill up with
a lot of darkness. It seemed to Jamie and Claudia that
they walked through miles of corridors. Fortunately,
the corridors were wide, and they were spared bumping into things.

At last they came to the hall of the English
Renaissance. Jamie quickly threw himself upon the
bed forgetting that it was only about six o'clock and
thinking that he would be so exhausted that he would
immediately fall asleep. He didn't. He was hungry.
That was one reason he didn't fall asleep immediately.
He was uncomfortable, too. So he got up from bed,
changed into his pajamas and got back into bed. He
felt a little better. Claudia had already changed into
her pajamas. She, too, was hungry, and she, too, was
uncomfortable. How could so elegant and romantic
a bed smell so musty? She would have liked to wash
everything in a good, strong, sweet-smelling detergent.

As Jamie got into bed, he still felt uneasy, and it
wasn't because he was worried about being caught.
Claudia had planned everything so well that he didn't
concern himself about that. The strange way he felt

had little to do with the strange place in which they were sleeping. Claudia felt it, too. Jamie lay there thinking. Finally, realization came.

"You know, Claude," he whispered, "I didn't brush my teeth."

Claudia answered, "Well, Jamie, you can't always brush after every meal." They both laughed very quietly. "Tomorrow," Claudia reassured him, "we'll be even better organized."

It was much earlier than her bedtime at home, but still Claudia felt tired. She thought she might have an iron deficiency anemia: tired blood. Perhaps, the pressures of everyday stress and strain had gotten her down. Maybe she was light-headed from hunger; her brain cells were being robbed of vitally needed oxygen for good growth and, and . . . yawn.

She shouldn't have worried. It had been an unusually busy day. A busy and unusual day. So she lay there in the great quiet of the museum next to the warm quiet of her brother and allowed the soft stillness to settle around them: a comforter of quiet. The silence seeped from their heads to their soles and into their souls. They stretched out and relaxed. Instead of oxygen and stress, Claudia thought now of hushed and quiet words: glide, fur, banana, peace. Even the footsteps of the night watchman added only an accented quarter-note to the silence that had become a hum, a lullaby.

They lay perfectly still even long after he passed.

Then they whispered good night to each other and fell asleep. They were quiet sleepers and hidden by the heaviness of the dark, they were easily not discovered.

(Of course, Saxonberg, the draperies of that bed helped, too.)

4

CLAUDIA AND JAMIE AWOKE VERY EARLY THE NEXT morning. It was still dark. Their stomachs felt like tubes of toothpaste that had been all squeezed out. Giant economy-sized tubes. They had to be out of bed and out of sight before the museum staff came on duty. Neither was accustomed to getting up so early, to feeling so unwashed, or feeling so hungry.

They dressed in silence. Each felt that peculiar chill that comes from getting up in the early morning. The chill that must come from one's own bloodstream, for it comes in summer as well as winter, from some inside part of you that knows it is early morning. Claudia always dreaded that brief moment when her pajamas were shed and her underwear was not yet on.

Even before she began undressing, she always had her underwear laid out on the bed in the right direction, right for getting into as quickly as possible. She did this now, too. But she hurried less pulling her petticoat down over her head. She took good long whiffs of the wonderful essence of detergent and clean dacron-cotton which floated down with the petticoat. Next to any kind of elegance, Claudia loved good clean smells.

After they were dressed, Claudia whispered to Jamie, "Let's stash our book bags and instrument cases before we man our stations."

They agreed to scatter their belongings. Thus, if the museum officials found one thing, they wouldn't necessarily find all. While still at home they had removed all identification on their cases as well as their clothing. Any child who has watched only one month's worth of television knows to do that much.

Claudia hid her violin case in a sarcophagus that had no lid. It was well above eye level, and Jamie helped hoist her up so that she could reach it. It was a beautifully carved Roman marble sarcophagus. She hid her book bag behind a tapestry screen in the rooms of French furniture. Jamie wanted to hide his things in a mummy case, but Claudia said that that would be unnecessarily complicated. The Egyptian wing of the Metropolitan was too far away from their bedroom; for the number of risks involved, it might as well be in Egypt. So the trumpet case was hidden inside a huge urn and Jamie's book bag was neatly tucked behind a drape that was behind a statue from the Middle Ages. Unfortunately, the museum people had fastened all the drawers of their furniture so that they couldn't be opened. They had never given a thought to the convenience of Jamie Kincaid.

"Manning their stations" meant climbing back into the booths and waiting during the perilous time when the museum was open to the staff but not to visitors. They washed up, combed their hair, and even brushed their teeth. Then began those long moments. That first morning they weren't quite sure when the staff would arrive, so they hid good and early. While Claudia stood crouched down waiting, the emptiness and the hollowness of all the museum corridors filled her stomach. She was starved. She spent her time trying not to remember delicious things to eat.

Jamie made one slight error that morning. It was almost enough to be caught. When he heard the sound of running water, he assumed that some male visitor was using the men's room to wash up. He checked his watch and saw that it was five past ten; he knew that the museum officially opened at ten o'clock, so he stepped down to walk out of his booth. It was not, however, a museum visitor who had turned on the water tap. It was a janitor filling his bucket. He was leaning down in the act of wringing out his mop when he saw Jamie's legs appear from nowhere and then saw Jamie emerge.

"Where did you come from?" he asked.

Jamie smiled and nodded. "Mother always says that I came from Heaven." He bowed politely and walked out, delighted with his brush with danger. He could hardly wait to tell Claudia. Claudia chose not to be amused on so empty a stomach.

The museum restaurant wouldn't open until eleven thirty and the snack bar wouldn't open until after that, so they left the museum to get breakfast. They went to the automat and used up a dollar's worth of Bruce's nickels. Jamie allotted ten nickels to Claudia and kept ten for himself. Jamie bought a cheese sandwich and coffee. After eating these he still felt hungry and told Claudia she could have twenty-five cents more for pie if she wished. Claudia, who had eaten cereal and drunk pineapple juice, scolded him about the need to eat properly. Breakfast food for breakfast, and lunch food for lunch. Jamie countered with complaints about Claudia's narrow-mindedness.

They were better organized that second day. Knowing that they could not afford more than two meals a day, they stopped at a grocery and bought small packages of peanut butter crackers for the night; they hid them in various pockets in their clothing. They decided to join a school group for lunch at the snack bar. There were certainly enough to choose from. That way their faces would always be just part of the crowd.

Upon their return to the museum, Claudia informed Jamie that they should take advantage of the wonderful opportunity they had to learn and to study. No other children in all the world since the world began had had such an opportunity. So she set forth for herself and for her brother the task of learning everything about the museum. One thing at a time. (Claudia probably didn't realize that the museum has over 365,000 works of art. Even if she had, she could not have been convinced that learning everything about everything was not possible; her ambitions were as enormous and as multi-directional as the museum itself.) Every day they would pick a different gallery about which they would learn everything. He could pick first. She would pick second; he, third; and so on. Just like the television schedule at home. Jamie considered learning something every day outrageous. It was not only outrageous; it was unnecessary. Claudia simply did not know how to escape. He thought he would put a quick end to this part of their runaway career. He chose the galleries of the Italian Renaissance. He didn't even know what the Renaissance was except that it sounded important and there seemed to be an awful lot of it. He figured that Claudia would soon give up in despair.

When she gave Jamie first pick, Claudia had been certain that he would choose Arms and Armor. She herself found these interesting. There was probably two days' worth of learning there. Perhaps, she might even choose the same on the second day.

MAIN FLOOR

E—Elevators
T—Toilets

INFORMATION DESK
879 5500 ext. 457

RESTAURANT HOURS:
Mondays Saturdays: 11 30 A M 2 30 P M
Sundays: 12 M 3 P M
COFFEE HOUR: Saturdays: 3 4 30 P M
Sundays: 3 30 4 30 P M

AMERICAN WING

ANCIENT NEAR EASTERN ART

EGYPTIAN ART

ARMS AND ARMOR

Oriental Armor

Ticket office

Grace Rainey Rogers Auditorium

Auditorium lounge

ENGLISH ARTS

Medieval Treasury

MEDIEVAL ART

Ancient Peruvian ceramics

EGYPTIAN ART

E

FRENCH ARTS

T

Library

Blumenthal Patio

Escalator

E

Recent accessions

Information

Membership office

Acoustiguide

Great Hall

Checkroom

Main entrance

Art and Book Shop

GREEK AND ROMAN ART

Color prints

E

T

Restaurant

SECOND FLOOR

E—Elevators
T—Toilets

EUROPEAN PAINTINGS AND SCULPTURE

AMERICAN WING

AMERICAN PAINTINGS AND SCULPTURE

ISLAMIC ART

FAR EASTERN ART.

ISLAMIC ART

ART OF INDIA

FAR EASTERN ART

20th c.

20th c.

19th c.

Dutch 17th c.

Flemish 17th c.

Spanish 17th c.

Italian 17th c.

French 17th c.

Dutch 17th c.

Bache collection

Rembrandt

Italian 18th c.

English 18th c.

Italian Renaissance

Italian and Spanish 14th c.

North-ern 15th c.

Italian 15th c.

Northern 15th 16th c.

Italian 16th c.

Altman collection

Chinese porcelains

French Sculpture

French 18th c.

David, Ingres, Goya

French 19th c.

French 19th c.

French 20th c.

French Impressionists

PRINTS AND DRAWINGS

Blumenthal Patio

Escalator

Print Study Room

Greek vases

Etruscan art

SPECIAL EXHIBITION GALLERIES

Claudia was surprised at Jamie's choice. But she thought she knew why he chose the Italian Renaissance. She thought she knew because along with tennis, ballet, and diving lessons at the "Y", she had taken art appreciation lessons last year. Her art teacher had said that the Renaissance was a period of glorification of the human form; as best she could figure out, that meant bare bodies. Many painters of the Italian Renaissance had painted huge billowy, bosomy naked ladies. She was amazed at Jamie; she thought he was too young for that. He was. She never even considered the possibility that he wanted her to be bored. She had given him first choice, and she was stuck with it. So she marched with him toward the long wide stairway straight in from the main entrance, which leads directly to the Hall of the Italian Renaissance.

If you think of doing something in New York City, you can be certain that at least two thousand other people have that same thought. And of the two thousand who do, about one thousand will be standing in line waiting to do it. That day was no exception. There were at least a thousand people waiting in line to see things in the Hall of the Italian Renaissance.

Claudia and Jamie did not think that there was anything unusual about the size of the crowd. This was New York. *Crowded* was part of the definition of New York. (To many art experts, Saxonberg, *crowded* is part of the definition of the Italian Renaissance, too. It was a time much like this: artistic activity was everywhere. Keeping track of the artists of the fifteenth and sixteenth centuries in Italy is as difficult as keeping track of the tax laws in the nineteen fifties and sixties in the United States. And almost as complicated.)

As they reached the top of the stairs, a guard said, "Line forms to the right. Single file, please." They did as they were told, partly because they didn't want to offend any guard or even attract his attention and partly because the crowd made them. Ladies' arms draped with pocketbooks and men's arms draped with coats formed a barrier as difficult to get through as barbed wire. Claudia and Jamie stood in the manner of all children who are standing in line. They stood leaning back with their necks stretched and their heads tilted away, way back, making a vain effort to see over the shoulders of the tall adult who always appears in front of them. Jamie could see nothing but the coat of the man in front of him. Claudia could see nothing but a piece of Jamie's head plus the coat of the man in front of Jamie.

They realized that they were approaching something out of the ordinary when they saw a newspaper cameraman walking along the edge of the crowd. The newsman carried a large, black, flash camera which had TIMES stencilled in white on its case. Jamie tried to slow down to the pace of the photographer. He didn't know what he was having his picture taken for, but he liked getting his picture taken—especially for a newspaper. Once when his class had visited the fire department, his picture had been in the paper at home. He had bought seven copies of the paper and used that page for bookcovers. When the bookcovers began to tear, he covered the covers with Saran wrap. They were still in his bookcase at home.

Claudia sensed danger. At least *she* remembered that they had run away from home, and she didn't want any New York paper advertising her whereabouts. Or Jamie's either. Especially if her parents happened to be looking for her. Someone in Greenwich was bound to read the *New York Times* and tell her folks. It would be more than a clue; it would be like booking anyone looking for them on a chartered bus ride straight to the hideaway. Wouldn't her brother ever learn inconspicuous? She shoved him.

He almost fell into the man in the coat. Jamie turned to Claudia and gave her an awful look. Claudia paid no attention, for now they reached what everyone was standing in line to see. A statue of an angel; her arms were folded, and she was looking holy. As Claudia passed by, she thought that that angel was the most beautiful, most graceful little statue she had ever seen; she wanted to stop and stare; she almost did, but the crowd wouldn't let her. As Jamie passed by, he thought that he would get even with Claudia for shoving him.

They followed the line to the end of the Renaissance Hall. When the velvet ropes that had guided
the crowd by creating a narrow street within the room
ended, they found themselves going down a staircase
to the main floor. Claudia was lost in remembrance
of the beautiful angel she had seen. Why did she
seem so important; and why was she so special? Of
course, she was beautiful. Graceful. Polished. But so
were many other things at the museum. Her sarcophagus, for example: the one in which her violin
case was hidden. And why was there all that commotion about her? The man had come to take pictures. There would be something about it in
tomorrow's paper. They could find out from the
newspapers.

She spoke to Jamie, "We'll have to buy a *New
York Times* tomorrow to see the picture."

Jamie was still mad about that shove. Why would
he want to buy the paper? He wouldn't be in the picture. He chose to fight Claudia with the one weapon
he had—the power of the purse. He answered, "We
can't afford a *New York Times*. It costs a dime."

"We've got to get one, Jamie. Don't you want to
know what's so important about that statue? Why
everyone is standing in line to see it?"

Jamie felt that letting Claudia know that she
couldn't get away with shoving him in public was
more important than his curiosity. "Well, perhaps,
tomorrow you can push someone down and grab his

paper while he's trying to get up. I'm afraid, though, that our budget won't allow this expense."

They walked for a short while before Claudia said, "I'll find out some way." She was determined about that.

She was also determined about learning; they wouldn't skip a lesson so easily. "Since we can't learn everything about the Italian Renaissance today, let's learn everything about the Egyptian rooms. That will be our lesson instead."

Jamie liked the mummies even if he didn't like lessons, so they walked together to the Egyptian wing. There they encountered a class that was also touring the halls. Each child in the class wore a round circle of blue construction paper on which was written in magic marker: Gr. 6, W.P.S. The class was seated on little rubber mats around a glass case within which was a mummy case within which was the mummy they were talking about. The teacher sat on a folding stool. Both Claudia and Jamie wandered over toward the class and soon became part of it—almost. They listened to the guide, a very pretty young lady who worked for the museum, and they learned a lot. They didn't even mind. They were surprised that they could actually learn something when they weren't in class. The guide told them how mummies were prepared and how Egypt's dry climate helped to preserve them. She told them about digging for tombs, and she told them about the beautiful princess Sit Hat-Hor Yunet whose jewelry they would see in another room. Before they left this room, however, she wanted to know if there were any questions. Since I'm sure this group was typical of all the school groups that I've observed at the museum, I can tell you what they were doing. At least twelve members of Gr. 6, W.P.S. were busy poking at each other. Twelve were wondering when they would eat; four were worried about how long it would be before they could get a drink of water.

Only Jamie had a question: "How much did it cost to become a mummy?"

The pretty guide thought he was part of the class; the teacher thought that he was planted in the audience to pep up the discussion; the class knew that he was an impostor. When they bothered to notice Claudia, they knew that she was one, also. But the class had the good manners that come with not caring; they would leave the impostors alone. The question, however, would have caused at least ten of them to stop poking at each other; six to forget about eating and three others to find the need for drink suddenly less urgent. It caused Claudia to want to embalm Jamie in a vat of mummy fluid right that minute. That would teach him *inconspicuous*.

The guide told Jamie that some people saved all their lives so that they could become mummies; it was indeed expensive.

One of the students called out, "You might even say it costs him his life."

Everyone laughed. Then they picked up their rubber mats and walked to the next room. Claudia was ready to pull Jamie out of line and make him learn another part of the museum today, but she got a glimpse of the room they were to go to next. It was filled with jewelry: case after case of it. So they followed the class into that hall. After a short talk there, the guide bid them good-bye and mentioned that they might enjoy buying some of the museum pamphlets on Egypt. Jamie asked if *they* were expensive.

The guide answered, "Some are as inexpensive as a copy of the Sunday *New York Times*. Others cost much more."

Jamie looked over at Claudia; he shouldn't have. Claudia looked as satisfied as the bronze statue of the Egyptian cat she was standing near. The only real difference between them was that the cat wore tiny golden earrings and looked a trifle less smug.

They got the *New York Times* the next day. Neither Claudia nor Jamie bought it. The man who left it on the counter while he was looking at the reproductions of antique jewelry bought it. The Kincaids stole it from him. They left the museum immediately thereafter.

Claudia read the paper while they ate breakfast at Horn and Hardart's. That morning she didn't eat breakfast food for breakfast. Crackers and roasted chestnuts in bed at night satisfied only a small corner

of her hunger. Being hungry was the most inconvenient part of running away. She meant to eat heartily for every cent Jamie gave her. She bought macaroni and cheese casserole, baked beans, and coffee that morning. Jamie got the same.

The information they wanted was on the first page of the second section of the *Times*. The headline said: RECORD CROWD VIEWS MUSEUM "BARGAIN." There were three pictures: one of the record crowd standing in line; one of the statue itself; and one of the director of the museum with an assistant. The article was as follows: (Saxonberg you can find an original of the newspaper in my files. It's in one of the seventeen cabinets that line the north wall of my office.)

Officials of the Metropolitan Museum of Art report that 100,000 people climbed the great stairway to catch a glimpse of one of its newest acquisitions, a twenty four inch statue called "Angel." Interest in the marble piece arises from the unusual circumstances attending its acquisition by the museum and from the belief that it may be the work of the Italian Renaissance master, Michelangelo. If proof is found that it is an early work of Michelangelo, the museum will have purchased the greatest bargain in art history; it was purchased at an auction last year for $225.00. Considering that recently Prince Franz Josef II accepted an offer of $5 million for a small painting by Leonardo da Vinci, an artist of the same period and of similar merit, will give some idea of how great a bargain this is.

The museum purchased the statue last year when one of its curators spotted it during a preview showing of works to be auctioned by the Parke-Bernet Galleries. His initial suspicion that it might be the work of Michelangelo was confirmed by several other museum officials, all of whom kept their thoughts quiet in a successful effort to keep the bidding from being driven higher. The statue has been the subject of exhaustive tests and study by the museum staff as well as art experts from abroad. Most believe it to have been done about 470 years ago when Michelangelo was in his early twenties.

The statue was acquired by the Parke-Bernet Galleries from the collection of Mrs. Basil E. Frankweiler. She claims to have purchased it from a dealer in Bologna, Italy before World War II. Mrs. Frankweiler's residence on East 63rd Street was long a Manhattan showplace for what many considered one of the finest private collections of art in the

Western Hemisphere. Others considered it a gigantic hodgepodge of the great and the mediocre. Mrs. Frankweiler closed her Manhattan residence three years ago; important pieces from its contents have found their way to various auctions and galleries since that time.

Mr. Frankweiler amassed a fortune from the corn oil industry and from developing many corn products. He died in 1947. Mrs. Frankweiler now lives on her country estate in Farmington, Connecticut. Her home, which at one time was open to the greats in the worlds of art, business, and politics, is now closed to all but her staff, her advisors, and a few close friends. The Frankweilers had no children.

A museum spokesman said yesterday, "Whether or not conclusive proof will be found that this was the work of Michelangelo, we are pleased with our purchase." Although Michelangelo Buonarroti is perhaps best known for his paintings of the Sistine Chapel in Rome, he always considered himself a sculptor, and primarily a sculptor of marble. The question of whether the museum has acquired one of his lesser known masterpieces still awaits a final answer."

If Claudia's interests had been a little broader, if she had started with the national news on page one and had then read the continuations on page twenty-eight, she might have noticed a small article on that page, one column wide, that would have interested her. The date line was Greenwich, Connecticut, and it stated that two children of Mr. and Mrs. Steven C. Kincaid, Sr. had been missing since Wednesday. The article didn't mention any clues like Claudia's letter. It said that the children were last seen wearing nylon quilted ski jackets. Small help. Fourteen out of fifteen kids in the U.S.A. wear those. It went on to describe Claudia as brunette and pretty and Jamie as brunette and brown eyed. Police in the neighboring towns of Darien and Stamford in Connecticut and Port Chester, New York, had been alerted. (You see, Saxonberg, Claudia had found the article about the statue too easily. She didn't even look at the first section of the paper. I keep telling you that often the search proves more profitable than the goal. Keep that in mind when you're looking for something in my files.)

Claudia and Jamie read about the statue with great interest. Claudia read the article twice so that she could memorize it all. She decided that the statue was not only the most beautiful in the world but also the most mysterious.

Jamie said, "I don't think $225 is cheap. I've never had that much money in my whole life. Totaling up all my birthday and Christmas presents since I was born nine long years ago wouldn't make $225.

Claudia said, "You wouldn't consider two and a quarter cents very much, would you?"

Jamie answered, "I might."

"That's right. *You* might, but most people wouldn't. Well, if this statue is by Michelangelo, it's worth about $2,250,000 instead of $225. That's the same as saying that suddenly two and a quarter cents is worth $225."

Jamie thought this over a minute. He was impressed. "When I grow up, I'm going to find a way to know for certain who did a statue."

This was all Claudia needed. Something that had been smoldering inside her since she first saw the statue, that had been fed by the *Times* article, now flared into an idea.

"Jamie, let's do it now. Let's skip learning everything about everything in the museum. Let's concentrate on the statue."

"Can we still take class tours as we did yesterday?"

Claudia answered, "Of course. We don't have to skip learning *something* about everything. We just won't learn everything about everything. We'll concentrate on Michelangelo."

Jamie snapped his fingers. "I've got it!" he exclaimed. He held up his hands for Claudia to see.

"What does that mean?"

"Fingerprints, silly. If Michelangelo worked on that statue, his fingerprints would be on it."

"Fingerprints? Almost five-hundred-year-old fingerprints? How would you know that they belonged to Michelangelo? He didn't have a police record. I don't suppose he did. As a matter of fact, I'm not sure people were fingerprinted in those days even if they did."

"But what if we were to find identical fingerprints on something they knew that he did? We could compare them."

Claudia kept looking at the picture of the statue as she finished eating her baked beans.

"Jamie," she said, "do you think the statue looks like anyone special?" She folded her arms and gazed into the distance.

"No one I know looks like an angel."

"Think a minute." She cleared her throat and lifted her chin slightly and gazed into the distance. "Don't think about the hair style or the clothes or anything. Just think about the face." She nudged the page of the *New York Times* closer under Jamie's nose and resumed her pose. Jamie looked at the picture.

"Nope," he said looking up.

"Can't you see any resemblance?"

"Nope." He looked at the picture again. "Who do you think it looks like?"

"Oh, I don't know," she stammered.

Jamie noticed Claudia blushing. "What's the matter? You getting a fever?"

"Don't be silly. I just feel that the statue looks like someone in our family."

"You sure you don't have a fever? You're talking out of your head."

Claudia unfolded her arms and lowered her distant gaze. "I wonder who posed for it," she said half aloud.

"Probably some fat old lady. Then the chisel slipped, so he made a skinny angel instead.

"Jamie, you have as much romance in you as the wolf in Little Red Riding Hood."

"Romance! Boloney! But I do like the mystery part."

"So do I!" Claudia answered. "But I like more than that about Angel."

"We going to look for fingerprints then?"

Claudia reconsidered, "Well, we might look for fingerprints. That's one way. For a start." She looked at Jamie and sniffed, "But I'm sure it won't work. We'll look tomorrow. Even though it won't work." And she looked some more at the picture.

On the second day the crowd going up the broad staircase to see the little Angel was even greater. The newspaper article had made people curious. Besides, it was a cloudy day, and museum attendance always improves in bad weather. Some people who had not been to the Metropolitan Museum for years came. Some people who had never been there ever, came; they got directions from maps, subway conductors, and police. (I'm surprised, Saxonberg, that seeing my name in the paper in connection with Michelangelo didn't bring even you to the museum. You would have profited more than you would have thought by that trip. Are photo albums of your grandchildren the only pictures you look at? Are you altogether unconscious of the magic of the name of Michelangelo? I truly believe that his name has magic even now; the best kind of magic because it comes from true greatness. Claudia sensed it as she again stood in line. The mystery only intrigued her; the magic trapped her.)

Both children were annoyed when the guards plus the push of the crowd hurried them past the Angel. How could they possibly look for fingerprints when they were so rushed? After this hurried visit to the statue, they decided to do their research when they had the statue and the museum to themselves. Claudia especially wanted to make herself important to the statue. She would solve its mystery; and it, in turn, would do something important to her, though what this was, she didn't quite know.

As they once again reached the back stairs, Claudia asked Jamie, "With whom shall we dine today, Sir James?"

"Jamie answered, "Oh, I don't know, dear Lady

Claudia. Shall we find a good and proper group?"

"Yes, let us, Sir James."

Thereupon, Jamie held out his arm, Claudia rested the tips of her fingers on the top of his hand, and they descended the stairs. They proved to be as fussy in their selection as Goldilocks. This group was too old; that group, too young; this, too small; that, all girls. But they found a good and proper group in the American wing where they spent a lovely and informative hour and a half learning about the arts and crafts of colonial days. They dined with the group, staying always at the rear of the line, always slightly apart. Both Jamie and Claudia had acquired a talent for being near but never part of a group. (Some people, Saxonberg, never learn to do that all their lives, and some learn it all too well.)

5

THEY HAD BEEN GONE FROM HOME FOR THREE DAYS now. Claudia insisted on a fresh change of underwear every day. That was the way she had been brought up. She insisted for Jamie, too. No question about it; their laundry was becoming a problem. They had to get to a laundromat. That night they removed all their dirty clothes from their instrument cases and stuffed those that would fit into various pockets. Those that didn't fit, they wore. A double layer of clothes never hurts anyone in winter, as long as the clean ones are worn closest to the skin.

Saturday seemed a good day for housekeeping chores. There would be no school groups for them to join. Claudia suggested that they eat both meals outside the museum. Jamie agreed. Claudia next suggested a real sit-down restaurant with tablecloths on the tables and waiters to serve you. Jamie said "NO" with such force that Claudia didn't try to persuade him.

From breakfast at the automat they went to laundry at the laundromat. They emptied their pockets of underwear and removed the layer of soiled socks. No one stared. Someone before them had probably done the same thing some time that week. They bought soap from a machine for ten cents and deposited a quarter into the slot in the washer. Through the glass in the door they watched their assorted clothing spill and splash over and over and around and around. Drying cost ten cents for ten minutes, but it took twenty cents worth of minutes to dry everything. When all was done, they were disappointed; all of it looked dismally gray. Very unelegant. Claudia had thought that their white underwear should not have been washed with the red and navy blue socks, but she would not have considered asking for more money for anything as unglamorous as dirty socks.

"Oh, well," she moaned, "at least they smell clean."

Jamie said, "Let's go to the TV department of Bloomingdale's and watch TV."

"Not today. We've got to work on the mystery of the statue all morning tomorrow, because tomor-

row the museum doesn't open until one o'clock. Today we must learn all about the Renaissance and
Michelangelo to prepare ourselves. We'll do research
at the big library at 42nd Street."

"How about the TV department of Macy's
instead?"

"To the library, Sir James."

"Gimbels?"

"Library."

They packed their gray-looking laundry back into
their pockets and walked to the door of the laundromat. At the door Claudia turned to Jamie and asked,
"Can we . . .?"

Jamie didn't let her finish, "No, dear Lady Claudia.
We have not the funds for taxis, buses, or subways.
"Shall we walk?" He extended his arm. Claudia
placed her gloved fingertips on top of Jamie's
mittened ones. Thus they began their long walk to
the library.

Once there, they asked the lady at the information booth where they could find books on Michelangelo. She directed them first to the children's room,
but when the librarian there found out what they
wanted to know, she advised them to go to the Don-
nell Branch Library on Fifty-third Street. Jamie hoped
this would discourage Claudia, but it didn't. She
didn't even seem to mind back-tracking up Fifth
Avenue. Her determination convinced Jamie that
Saturday should be spent just this way. Once at the

library, they examined the directory which told what was available where and when the library was open. In the downstairs Art Room the librarian helped them find the books which Claudia selected from the card catalogue. She even brought them some others. Claudia liked that part. She always enjoyed being waited on.

Claudia began her studies never doubting that she could become an authority that morning. She had neither pencil nor paper to make notes. And she knew she wouldn't have a lot of time to read. So she decided that she would simply remember everything, absolutely everything she read. Her net profit, therefore, would be as great as that of someone who read a great deal but remembered very little.

Claudia showed the executive ability of a corporation president. She assigned to Jamie the task of looking through the books of photographs of Michelangelo's work to find pictures of Angel. She would do the reading. She glanced through several thick books with thin pages and tiny print. After reading twelve pages, she looked to the end to see how many more pages there were to go: more than two hundred. The book also had footnotes. She read a few more pages and then busied herself with studying some of Jamie's picture books.

"You're supposed to do the reading!"

"I'm just using these pictures for relief," Claudia whispered. "I have to rest my eyes sometime."

"Well, I don't see any pictures that look like that statue," Jamie sighed.

"Keep looking. I'll do some more reading."

A few minutes later Jamie interrupted her. "Here he is," he said.

"That doesn't look anything like the statue. That's not even a girl," Claudia said.

"Of course not. That's Michelangelo himself."

Claudia replied, "I knew that."

"Two minutes ago you didn't. You thought I was showing you a picture of the statue."

"Oh, I meant . . . I meant. Well . . . there's his broken nose." She pointed to the nose in the picture. "He got in a fight and had his nose broken when he was a teenager."

"Was he a juvenile delinquent? Maybe they do have his fingerprints on file."

"No, silly," Claudia said. "He was a hot-tempered genius. Did you know he was famous even when he was alive?"

"Is that so? I thought that artists don't become famous until after they're dead. Like mummies."

They studied a while longer before Jamie's next interruption. "You know, a lot of his works were lost. They say *lost* in parentheses under the picture."

"How can that be? A statue isn't something like an umbrella that you leave in a taxi and lose. That is, those people who actually ride taxis; something you wouldn't know about."

"Well, they weren't lost in taxis. They were lost track of."

"What kind of a sentence is that? Lost track of?"

"Oh, boloney! There are whole long books about the lost works of Michelangelo. Picture works and sculptor works that people lost track of."

Claudia softened. "Is the little angel one of them?"

"What's the difference between an angel and a cupid?" Jamie inquired.

"Why?" Claudia asked.

"Because there's a lost cupid for sure."

"Angels wear clothes and wings and are Christian. Cupids wear bows and arrows; they are naked and pagan."

"What's pagan?" Jamie asked. "Boy or girl?"

"How would I know?" Claudia answered.

"You said they are naked."

"Well, pagan has nothing to do with that. It means worshipping idols instead of God."

"Oh," Jamie nodded. "The statue in the museum is an angel. It's dressed in its altogether. I don't know yet if an angel was lost . . ." Then he glanced over at his sister and muttered, "track of."

Claudia had begun her research confident that a morning's study would make her completely an expert; but Michelangelo had humbled her, and humility was not an emotion with which she felt comfortable; she was irritable. Jamie ended his research where Claudia had begun: very confident and happy. He felt that his morning had been well spent; he had seen a lot of pictures and he had learned about pagan. He leaned back and yawned; he was becoming bored with pictures of David and Moses and the Sistine Ceiling; he wanted to find clues. Already he knew enough to tell if Michelangelo had sculptured the little angel. All he needed was a chance to investigate. Without the guards hurrying him. He would know, but would his opinion be accepted by the experts?

"I think we should find out how the experts decide whether or not the statue belongs to Michelangelo. That will be better than finding out about Michelangelo himself," Jamie said.

"I know how they find out. They gather evidence like sketches he did and diaries and records of sales. And they examine the statue to see what kind of tools were used and how they were used. Like no one living in the fifteenth century would use an electric drill. How come you didn't take art appreciation lessons with me?"

"The summer before last?"

"Yes. Before school started."

"Well, the summer before last, I had just finished the second half of first grade."

"So what?"

"So boloney! It was all I could do to sound out the name of Dick and Jane's dog."

Claudia had no answer for Jamie's logic. Besides, Jamie agreed with her, "I guess it is better to look for clues. After all, we're doing something that none of the experts can do."

Claudia's impatience surfaced. She had to pick a fight with Jamie. "Don't be silly. They can read all this stuff, too. There's certainly plenty of it."

"Oh, I don't mean that. I mean that we're living with the statue. You know what they always say: The only two ways to get to know someone are to live with him or play cards with him."

"Well, at least the little statue can't cheat at cards like someone else I know."

"Claudia, dear, I'm no angel. Statue or otherwise."

Claudia sighed, "O.K. Sir James, let's go." And they did.

As they were walking up the steps, Jamie spied a Hershey's almond bar still in its wrapper lying in the corner of the landing. He picked it up and tore open one corner.

"Was it bitten into?" asked Claudia.

"No," Jamie smiled. "Want half?"

"You better not touch it," Claudia warned. "It's probably poisoned or filled with marijuana, so you'll eat it and become either dead or a dope addict."

Jamie was irritated. "Couldn't it just happen that someone dropped it?"

"I doubt that. Who would drop a whole candy bar and not know it? That's like leaving a statue in a taxi. Someone put it there on purpose. Someone who pushes dope. I read once that they feed dope in chocolates to little kids, and then the kids become dope addicts, then these people sell them dope at very high prices which they just can't help but buy because when you're addicted you have to have your dope. High prices and all. And Jamie, we don't have that kind of money."

Jamie said, "Oh, well, bottoms up." He took a big bite of the candy, chewed and swallowed. Then he closed his eyes, leaned against the wall and slid to the floor. Claudia stood with her mouth open, stunned. She was on the verge of screaming for help when Jamie opened his eyes and smiled. "It's delicious. Want a bite?"

Claudia not only refused the bite, she also refused to talk to Jamie until they got to the restaurant. Lunch cheered her. She suggested that they play in Central Park for a while, and they did. They bought peanuts, chestnuts, and pretzels from the vendor outside the museum. They knew that since the museum opened late on Sunday, they would accumulate a lot of hunger before they got out. Their bulging pockets were now full of the staples of life: food and clothing.

Jamie entered the men's room. He had arrived, as was his custom, shortly before the first bell rang, the bell that warned everyone that the museum would close in five minutes. He waited; the bell rang. He got into a booth. First bell, second bell, it was routine just as boarding the school bus had once been routine. After the first day, they had learned that the staff worked from nine A.M. until five P.M., a work schedule just like their father's. Routine, routine. The wait from nine when the staff came until ten when the public came seemed long. Claudia and Jamie had decided that the washrooms were good for the shorter evening wait when the help left at the same time as the visitors, but the washrooms were less satisfactory for the long morning wait . . . especially after Jamie's close call that first morning. So time from eight forty-five until some safe time after ten in the mornings was spent under various beds. They always checked for dust under the bed first. And for once Claudia's fussiness was not the reason. Reason was the reason. A dustless floor meant that it had been cleaned very recently, and they stood less chance of being caught by a mop.

Jamie stood on the toilet seat waiting. He leaned his head against the wall of the booth and braced himself for what would happen next. The guard would come in and make a quick check of his station. Jamie still felt a ping during that short inspection; that was the only part that still wasn't quite routine, and that's why he braced himself. Then the lights would be turned out. Jamie would wait twelve minutes (lag time, Claudia called it) and emerge from hiding.

Except.

Except the guard didn't come, and Jamie couldn't

relax until after he felt that final ping. And the lights stayed on, stayed on. Jamie checked his watch ten times within five minutes; he shook his arm and held the watch up to his ear. It was ticking slower than his heart and much more softly. What was wrong? They had caught Claudia! Now they would look for him! He'd pretend he didn't speak English. He wouldn't answer any questions.

Then he heard the door open. Footsteps. More footsteps than usual. What was happening? The hardest part was that every corpuscle of Jamie's nine-year-old self was throbbing with readiness to run, and he had to bind up all that energy into a quiet lump. It was like trying to wrap a loose peck of potatoes into a neat four-cornered package. But he managed to freeze. He heard the voices of two men talking over the sound of water running in the sink.

"I guess they expect even more people tomorrow."

"Yeah. Sundays are always jammed up anyway."

"It'll be easier to move the people in and out of the Great Hall."

"Yeah. Two feet of marble. What do you figure it weighs?"

"I dunno. Whatever it weighs, it has to be handled delicate. Like it was a real angel."

"C'mon. They probably have the new pedestal ready. We can start."

"Do you think they'll have as many people as they had for the Mona Lisa?"

"Naw! The Mona Lisa was here for a short time only. Besides it was the real McCoy."

"I think this one's . . ."

The men left, turning off the lights as they did so. Jamie heard the door close before he melted. Legs first. He sat down on the seat as he allowed the familiar darkness as well as new realization to fill him.

They were moving Angel. Did Claudia know? They wouldn't have women moving the statue. There would be no one in the ladies' room washing up. Who would give her the information? He would. By mental telepathy. He would think a message to Claudia. He folded his hands across his forehead and concentrated. "Stay put, Claudia, stay put. Stay put. Stay put. Claudia, stay put." He thought that Claudia would not approve of the grammar in his mental telegram; she would want him to think *stay in place*. But he didn't want to weaken his message by varying it one bit. He continued thinking STAY PUT.

He must have thought STAY PUT exactly hard enough, for Claudia did just that. They never knew exactly why she did, but she did. Perhaps she sensed some sounds that told her that the museum was not yet empty. Maybe she was just too tired from running around in Central Park. Maybe they were not meant to get caught. Maybe they were meant to make the discovery they made.

They waited for miles and miles of time before they came out of hiding. At last they met in their bedroom. Claudia was sorting the laundry when Jamie got there. In the dark, mostly by feel. Although there is no real difference between boys' stretch socks and girls', neither ever considered wearing the other's. Children who have always had separate bedrooms don't.

Claudia turned when she heard Jamie come up and said, "They moved the statue."

"How did you know? Did you get my message?"

"Message? I saw the statue on my way here. They have a dim light on it. I guess so that the night guard won't trip over it."

Jamie replied, "We're lucky we didn't get caught."

Claudia never thought very hard about the plus-luck she had; she concentrated on the minus-luck. "But they held us up terribly. I planned on our taking baths tonight. I really can't stand one night more without a bath."

"I don't mind," Jamie said.

"Come along, Sir James. To our bath. Bring your most elegant pajamas. The ones embroidered in gold with silver tassels will do."

"Where, dear Lady Claudia, dost thou expect to bathe?"

"In the fountain, Sir James. In the fountain."

Jamie extended his arm, which was draped with his striped flannel pajamas, and said, "Lady Claudia, I knew that sooner or later you would get me to that restaurant."

(It makes me furious to think that I must explain that restaurant to you, Saxonberg. I'm going to make you take me to lunch in there one day soon. I just this minute became determined to get you into the museum. You'll see later how I'm going to do it. Now about the restaurant. It is built around a gigantic fountain. Water in the fountain is sprayed from dolphins sculptured in bronze. The dolphins appear to be leaping out of the water. On their backs are figures representing the arts, figures that look like water sprites. It is a joy to sit around that wonderful fountain and to snack petit fours and sip expresso coffee. I'll bet that you'd even forget your blasted ulcer while you ate there.)

Lady Claudia and Sir James quietly walked to the entrance of the restaurant. They easily climbed under the velvet rope that meant that the restaurant was closed to the public. Of course they were not the public. They shed their clothes and waded into the fountain. Claudia had taken powdered soap from the restroom. She had ground it out into a paper towel that morning. Even though it was freezing cold, she enjoyed her bath. Jamie, too, enjoyed his bath. For a different reason.

When he got into the pool, he found bumps on the bottom; smooth bumps. When he reached down to feel one, he found that it moved! He could even pick it up. He felt its cool roundness and splashed his

way over to Claudia. "Income, Claudia, income!" he whispered.

Claudia understood immediately and began to scoop up bumps she had felt on the bottom of the fountain. The bumps were pennies and nickels people had pitched into the fountain to make a wish. At least four people had thrown in dimes and one had tossed in a quarter.

"Some one very rich must have tossed in this quarter," Jamie whispered.

"Some one very poor," Claudia corrected. "Rich people have only penny wishes."

Together they collected $2.87. They couldn't hold more in their hands. They were shivering when they got out. Drying themselves as best they could with paper towels (also taken from the restroom), they hurried into their pajamas and shoes.

They finished their preparations for the night, took a small snack and decided it was safe to wander back into the Great Hall to look again at their Angel.

"I wish I could hug her," Claudia whispered.

"They probably bugged her already. Maybe that light is part of the alarm. Better not touch. You'll set it off."

"I said 'hug' not 'bug!' Why would I want to bug her?"

"That makes more sense than to hug her."

"Silly. Shows how much you know. When you hug someone, you learn something else about them.

An important something else."

Jamie shrugged his shoulders.

Both looked at Angel a long time. "What do you think?" Jamie asked. "Did he or didn't he?"

Claudia answered, "A scientist doesn't make up his mind until he's examined all the evidence."

"You sure don't sound like a scientist. What kind of scientist would want to hug a statue?"

Claudia was embarrassed, so she spoke sternly, "We'll go to bed now, and we'll think about the statue very hard. Don't fall asleep until you've really thought about the statue and Michelangelo and the entire Italian Renaissance."

And so they went to bed. But lying in bed just before going to sleep is the worst time for *organized* thinking; it is the best time for free thinking. Ideas drift like clouds in an undecided breeze, taking first this direction and then that. It was very difficult for Jamie to control his thoughts when he was tired, sleepy, and lying on his back. He never liked to get involved just before falling asleep. But Claudia had planned on their thinking, and she was good at planning. So think he did. Clouds bearing thoughts of the Italian Renaissance drifted away. Thoughts of home, and more thoughts of home settled down.

"Do you miss home?" he asked Claudia.

"Not too much," she confessed. "I haven't thought about it much."

Jamie was quiet for a minute, then he said, "We

probably have no conscience. I think we ought to be homesick. Do you think Mom and Dad raised us wrong? They're not very mean, you know; don't you think that should make us miss them?"

Claudia was silent. Jamie waited. "Did you hear my question, Claude?"

"Yes. I heard your question. I'm thinking." She was quiet a while longer. Then she asked, "Have you ever been homesick?"

"Sure."

"When was the last time?"

"That day Dad dropped us off at Aunt Zell's when he took Mom to the hospital to get Kevin."

"Me, too. That day," Claudia admitted. "But, of course, I was much younger then."

"Why do you suppose we were homesick that day? We've been gone much longer than that now."

Claudia thought. "I guess we were worried. Boy, had I known then that she was going to end up with Kevin, I would have known why we were worried. I remember you sucked your thumb and carried around that old blanket the whole day. Aunt Zell kept trying to get the blanket away from you so that she could wash it. It stank."

Jamie giggled, "Yeah, I guess homesickness is like sucking your thumb. It's what happens when you're not very sure of yourself."

"Or not very well trained," Claudia added. "Heaven knows, we're well trained. Just look how nicely we've managed. It's really their fault if we're not homesick."

Jamie was satisfied. Claudia was more. "I'm glad you asked that about homesickness, Jamie. Somehow, I feel older now. But, of course, that's mostly because I've been the oldest child forever. And I'm extremely well adjusted."

They went to sleep then. Michelangelo, Angel, and the entire Italian Renaissance waited for them until morning.

6

It was still dark when they awoke the next morning, but it was later than usual. The museum wouldn't open until one. Claudia was up first. She was getting dressed when Jamie opened his eyes.

"You know," he said, "Sunday is still Sunday. It *feels* like Sunday. Even here."

Claudia answered, "I noticed that. Do you think we ought to try to go to church when we go out?"

Jamie thought a minute before answering, "Well, let's say a prayer in that little room of the Middle Ages. The part with the pretty stained glass window."

They dressed and walked to the little chapel and knelt and said *The Lord's Prayer*. Jamie reminded Claudia to say she was sorry for stealing the newspaper. That made it officially Sunday.

"C'mon," Claudia said as she was rising, "let's go to the statue."

They walked over to Angel and looked very closely. It was difficult to look for clues. Even after their research. They were accustomed to having all the clues neatly laid out on a diagram placed in front of the exhibit.

"I still say that it's too bad we can't touch her," Claudia complained.

"At least we're living with it. We're the only two people in the whole world who live with it."

"Mrs. Frankweiler did, too. She could touch . . ."

"And hug it," Jamie teased.

"I'll bet she knows for sure if Michelangelo did it."

"Sure she does," Jamie said. He then threw his arms around himself, leaned his head way back, closed his eyes, and murmured, "Every morning when she got up, Mrs. Frankweiler would throw her arms about the statue, peer into its eyes, and say, 'speak to me, baby.' One morning the statue ans . . ."

Claudia was furious. "The men who moved it last night hugged it when they moved it. There's all kinds of hugging."

She refused to look at Jamie again and instead stared at the statue. The sound of footsteps broke the silence and her concentration. Footsteps from the Italian Renaissance were descending upon them! The guard was coming down the steps. Oh, boloney!

thought Jamie. There was just too much time before the museum opened on Sundays. They should have been in hiding already. Here they were out in the open with a light on!

Jamie grabbed Claudia's hand and pulled her behind the booth where they rent walkie-talkies for a tour of the museum. Even though they were well hidden by the dark as they squatted there, they felt as exposed as that great bare lady in the painting upstairs.

The footsteps stopped in front of Angel. Jamie sent another mental telegram: Get going, get going, get going. Of course it worked. The guard moved on toward the Egyptian wing to cover the rest of his tour. The two children wouldn't even allow themselves a sigh of relief. They were that well disciplined.

After ten minutes lag time, Jamie tugged the hem of Claudia's jacket, and they cautiously got up. Jamie led the way back up the great stairway. As he did so, his logic became clear to Claudia. Thank goodness Jamie thought so clearly so fast, and thank goodness for those twenty acres of floor space. It would take the watchman more than an hour before he passed that way again.

They stealthily climbed the wide stairway, staying close to the rail. Step, pause. Step, pause. All the way to the top until they found themselves in front of the pedestal on which Angel had stood just the day before. Claudia paused to look; partly from habit and partly because anything associated with Angel was precious. Jamie paused to catch his breath.

"Why do you think they changed the velvet under her from blue to gold?" Claudia whispered.

This blue probably got dirty. C'mon, let's hide."

Claudia looked again at the velvet. Light was beginning to seep into the museum. Something on top of the velvet caught her eye. "One of the workmen must have been drinking beer when he moved the statue."

"Most people drink beer," Jamie said. "What's so unusual about that?"

"They don't let visitors bring in beer," answered Claudia. "I wonder why they allow the workers to do it? What if he had spilled it on Angel? See where he must have put his beer can on that platform." She pointed to the blue velvet covering the pedestal. "See the rings where the pile of the velvet isn't crushed."

Jamie said, "Yeah, Ballantine beer. Those three rings." Then he began humming a commercial that he had heard during the baseball game on television last spring.

Claudia interrupted, "Those are the marks of the beer can itself. After all, the emblem on the can is flat against the can. It could have been any kind of beer. Schlitz, Rheingold."

Jamie stared at the blue velvet. "You're right, Claude. Except for one thing."

"What's that?" she asked.

"The rings the beer cans made would have crushed the plush of the velvet *down* . . . and the plush of this velvet is crushed *up*."

"What kind of a sentence is that? Crushed *up*!"

"Oh, boloney! You just go ahead and pick on my grammar. Go ahead pick on my grammar. But you can't pick on my logic. The weight of the statue crushed all the velvet down except where the marble was chipped away and the plush was crushed up. Claudia, there's a crushed-up W in one of those circles that is also crushed up."

"For goodness' sake, Jamie. That's not a W; that's an M." She looked at Jamie, and her eyes widened, "M for Michelangelo!"

Jamie was rubbing his eyes. "You know, Claude, I saw that symbol yesterday on the cover of one of the books I looked at."

"What was it, Jamie? What was it?"

"How should I know? You were supposed to be doing the reading! I was just supposed to be looking for pictures and clues."

"James Kincaid, you are *something*. You are *absolutely* something. As if it would have hurt you to read one little thing. Just one little thing!"

Jamie said, "Well, we have a clue."

"We could know already."

"We have an important clue. I'll bet they never even looked at the bottom of the statue."

"Now we have to go back to the library today to find out what that symbol means. But we can't! That library is closed on Sundays. Oh, Jamie, I've got to know."

"We'll check the museum bookshop. Don't worry, Claude; I'll recognize the book. Right now, we better hide."

Claudia glanced at her watch. "Where are we going to hide up here? There's no furniture. We can't risk going downstairs again."

Jamie picked up a corner of the blue velvet drape. "Be my guest," he said indicating the floor under the platform with an elegant sweep of his hand.

Jamie and Claudia squatted under the platform waiting. It was close quarters under there. Jamie needed only to point his fingers to poke his sister in the ribs. "I say, Lady Claudia, I do believe we're safe and onto something really great."

"Perhaps, Sir James, perhaps."

Claudia didn't think about their close calls. They were unimportant; they wouldn't matter in the end, the end having something to do with Michelangelo, Angel, history, and herself. She thought about the history test she had had on Monday at school. There had been a question on the test that she couldn't answer. She had studied hard and read the chapter thoroughly. She knew where the answer was—the second paragraph in the right hand column of page 157. In her mind she could actually see *where* the *answer* was, but she couldn't think of *what* it was.

Angel was that way. An answer to running away, and also to going home again, lay in Angel. She knew it was there, but she didn't know what it was. It was just escaping her as the answer to the question on the test had . . . except this was even harder, for she wasn't exactly certain of the question she was trying to answer. The question had something to do with why Angel had become more important than having run away or even being safe, at the museum. Oh! she was right back where she had started. It was too stuffy under that velvet. How could anyone think straight? No wonder her thinking came out in circles. She knew one thing for sure: maybe they had a clue.

A crowd formed in front of the museum before it opened. The guard who was to have removed the pedestal and drape was called outside to set up sawhorses and make orderly rows out of the mass of people. The museum couldn't spare Morris until after the police had sent help for the sidewalk traffic. When he finally moved the platform and drape and took them to the basement for storage, Claudia and Jamie had already left and were browsing around the crowded bookshop peeking under the dust jackets of books about Michelangelo.

They found the book with the mark on the cover! The crushed-up mark on the dark blue velvet was

Michelangelo's stonemason's mark. He had chipped
it into the base of the marble to identify himself as
owner, much as brands are burned into the hides of
cattle to identify their owners.

They emerged from the bookshop feeling triumphant. And hungry.

"C'mon," Claudia shouted as soon as they got
out, "Let's grab a taxi to the Automat."

"We'll walk," Jamie said.

"We have income now. All we have to do is take
a bath whenever we need money."

Jamie thought a second. "O.K. I'll allow a bus."

Claudia smiled. "Thank you, Mr. Pinchpenny."

"You call me Pinchpenny, and I'll call you . . ."

"Call me a taxi," she laughed, running toward the
bus stop in front of the museum.

Jamie was feeling so satisfied that he gave Claudia
seventy-five cents for brunch. He allowed himself the
same. As they ate, they discussed what they should do
about the awesome information they had.

"Let's call the *New York Times*," Jamie suggested.
All that publicity! They'll want to know how we
found out."

"Let's call the head of the Metropolitan."

"*He'll* want to know how we found out."

"We'll tell him," Jamie said.

"Are you out of your mind?" Claudia asked. "Tell
him we've been living there?"

"Don't you think we ought to tell the museum about the crushed-up mark on the velvet?"

"We owe it to them," Claudia answered. "We've been their guests all this time."

"Then you figure out how we can let them know without getting caught. I'll bet you already have it all worked out."

"As a matter of fact, I do." Claudia leaned across the table and spoke to Jamie in her best secret agent fashion. "We'll write them a letter and tell them to look at the base of the statue for an important clue."

"What if they can't figure out what the clue is?"

"We'll help them with that when they need help. We'll reveal ourselves then. And they'll be very happy to have been our hosts," Claudia said. She paused long enough for Jamie to begin to get impatient, but just begin. "Here's the plan: we rent a post office box in Grand Central. Like when you send in box tops, you always send them to P.O. Box Number So-and-so. We write a letter and tell them to answer us at the box number. After they tell us that they need help, we reveal ourselves. As heroes."

"Can't we go home and wait? That was rough last night and this morning. Besides, then we can be heroes twice. Once when we return home and once when we reveal ourselves."

"No!" Claudia screeched. "We have to know about Angel first. We have to be right."

"Wow! What's the matter with you, Claude? You know you planned on going home sometime."

"Yes," she answered, "sometime. But not just anytime." Her voice was becoming high pitched again.

"Anytime we come home—from a visit to Grandpa's or from summer camp—they're always glad to see us."

"But it never makes any difference. Going home without knowing about Angel for sure will be the same as going home from camp. It won't be any different. After one day, maybe two, we'll be back to the same old thing. And I didn't run away to come home the same."

"Well, this has been more fun than camp. Even the food's been better. There's that difference."

"But, Jamie, it's not enough."

"Yeah, I know, it's not enough. I'm hungry most of the time."

"I mean the difference is not enough. Like being born with perfect pitch, or being born very ordinary and then winning the Congressional Medal of Honor or getting an Academy Award. Those are differences that will last a lifetime. Finding out about Angel will be that kind of difference.

"I think you're different already, Claude."

"Do you?" she asked. She was smiling and her eyes were modestly lowered, ready for a compliment.

"Yes. We're all sane, and you're *insane*."

"Jamie Kincaid!"

"O.K. O.K. I'm insane, too. I'll go along with you. Besides some of the complications are getting interesting, even though some are dull. How will you disguise your handwriting?"

"No need to do that. I'll use a typewriter." Claudia waited for Jamie's look of surprise.

She got it. "Where are you going to get a typewriter?"

"In front of the Olivetti place on Fifth Avenue. We passed it twice yesterday. Once when you made us walk from the laundromat. And again when we walked from library to library. It's bolted to a stand outside the building for everyone to use. You know, sort of a sample of their product. It's free."

Jamie smiled, "It's a good thing that I'm insane about walking. Otherwise, you would never have found that typewriter."

"And it's a good thing that I'm an excellent observer," Claudia added.

They marched up Fifth Avenue and were delighted to find a piece of paper already in the typewriter. Across the top of the page someone had typed: Now is the time for all good men to come to the aid of their party. Claudia didn't know that this sentence was a common one used in practice typing. She thought it appeared appropriate to their message and would add a proper note of mystery besides. (Here,

Saxonberg, is a copy of the letter Claudia typed. You
can see that her typing needed a great deal of
improvement.)

> Now is the time for all good men to come to
> the aid of their party;

Dear Museum Head,
    We think that you should examine the
bottom of the statue for an important clue.
The statue we mean is the one you bought for
$225.00. And the clue is that you will find
Michelangelo's stone mason's mark on the
bottom. If you need help about this clue, you
may write to us at Grand Central Post Office.
Box 847 in Manhanttan.
                    Sincerely,
                Friends of the Museum

Pleased with their effort, they felt that they could
take the rest of the day off. They wandered around
Rockefeller Center and watched the skaters for a short
while. They watched the crowd watching the skaters
for a while longer. When they returned to the museum filled with satisfaction and with snacks for their
supper, they saw a long line of Sunday people waiting
to climb the museum steps. Knowing that everyone
in that line would be shepherded in and out, in front
of and past the statue in a matter of minutes, they

decided to enter through the rear entrance instead. The guard at that door told them that they would have to use the Fifth Avenue entrance if they wished to see Angel.

"Oh, we've already seen that!" Jamie said.

The guard from friendliness, helpfulness or, perhaps, sheer loneliness (very few people had entered through his door that day) asked Jamie what he thought of it.

"Well, we need to do more research, but it seems to me that . . ."

Claudia pulled Jamie's arm. "Come along, *Albert*," she urged.

On their way to the rooms containing Greek vases, they again observed the enormous crowd passing by the statue.

"As I was about to tell that guard, it seems to me that they should try to get to the *bottom* of the mystery."

Claudia giggled; Jamie joined in. They spent exactly enough time among the vases of ancient Greece to be able to man their waiting stations and not be discovered.

7

When they left the museum on Monday morning, Claudia walked to the bus stop without even consulting Jamie.

"Don't you think we ought to get breakfast first?" He asked.

"Mail early in the day," Claudia answered. "Besides, we want them to get this letter as soon as possible."

"It will get there faster if we deliver it by hand," Jamie suggested.

"Good idea. We'll get our mailbox number, write it in, and then take it to the museum office."

Since Jamie was official treasurer of the team, it

was he who approached the man behind the cage window at the post office.

"I would like to rent a post office box," he declared.

"For how long?" the man inquired.

"For about two days."

"Sorry," the man said, "we rent them quarterly."

"All right, then. I'll take eight quarterlies. That makes two days."

"Quarter of a year," the man said. "That makes three months."

"Just a minute," Jamie said. He held a whispered conference with Claudia.

"Go ahead. Rent it," she urged.

"It'll cost a stack of money."

"Why don't you find out instead of arguing about it now?" Claudia's whisper began to sound like cold water hitting a hot frying pan.

"How much will a quarter of a year be?" he asked the postman.

"Four dollars and fifty cents."

Jamie scowled at Claudia. "See. I told you a stack."

Claudia shrugged her shoulders, "We'll take a long, long bath tonight."

The postman hardly looked puzzled. People working at the Grand Central Post Office grow used to strange remarks. They hear so many. They never stop hearing them; they simply stop sending the messages to their brains. Like talking into a telephone with no one on the receiver end. "Do you or don't you want it?" he asked.

"I'll take it."

Jamie paid the rent, signed a form using the name Angelo Michaels and gave his address as Marblehead, Massachusetts. He received a key to Box Number 847. Jamie-Angelo-Kincaid-Michaels felt important having a key to his own mailbox. He found his box and opened the little door.

"You know," he remarked to Claudia, "it's a lot like Horn and Hardart's. Except that we could have a complete spaghetti dinner for both of us coming out of the little door instead of just empty, empty space.

Paying four dollars and fifty cents for empty space had been hard on Jamie. Claudia knew they wouldn't take a bus back to the museum. They didn't.

Both Claudia and Jamie wanted to deliver the letter, but neither thought he should. Too risky. They decided to ask someone to deliver it for them. Someone with a bad memory for faces. Someone their own age would be best; someone who might be nosey but who wouldn't really care about them. It would be easiest to find a school group and select their messenger. They began their search for the group of the day by looking in the usual places: Arms and Armor, the Costume Institute, and Egyptian Art. As they approached the Egyptian wing, they heard the shuffling of feet and a sound they recognized as the folding of chairs and the gathering up of rubber mats. They weren't anxious to hear the talk about mummies again; they never watched repeats on television, either. But they decided to look the group over. So they waited inside the tomb.

(Now, Saxonberg, I must tell you about that Egyptian tomb called a mastaba. It is not a whole one; it is the beginning of one. You can walk into it. You can spend a lot of time in it, or you can spend very little time in it. You can try to read the picture writing on the walls. Or you can read nothing at all. Whether you read or not, whether you spend a lot of time or a little in that piece of Ancient Egypt, you will have changed climate for at least that part of your day. It is not a hard place to wait in at all.)

The group was moving past the entrance. Claudia and Jamie were relaxed and waiting—wrapped up in the vacuum of time created by those warm stone walls. Puffs of conversation broke the silence of their tomb.

"Sarah looks like pharaoh. Pass it on."

"When are we gonna eat?"

"Man, what a lot of walking."

The conversation rained in softly and comfortably and told the two stowaways that they had the correct age group. That was the way kids in their classes always talked. Words continued to drizzle into their shelter.

"Hey, Rube, look at this."

"C'mon, Bruce, let me borrow it."

Something else now showered down upon them. Something much less comfortable. *Familiarity!* The names, Sarah, Bruce, Rube, were familiar . . . Ages ago, in time well outside the mastaba, they had heard these names—in a classroom, on a school bus . . .

Closer, louder, the sounds poured in. Then one small cloud burst right outside their door.

"Hey, let's go back in here."

Jamie's eyes caught Claudia's. He opened his mouth. Claudia didn't wait to discover whether he opened it in surprise or to say something. She clamped her hand over his mouth as fast as she could.

An adult voice urged, "Come on, boys. We have to stay with the group."

Claudia took her hand from Jamie's mouth. She looked at him solemnly and nodded *yes*. The "come-on-boys" voice belonged to Miss Clendennan, Jamie's third grade teacher. Rube was Reuben Hearst, and Bruce was Bruce Lansing. Sarah was Sarah Sawhill, and unfortunately, she did look a great deal like pharaoh. Believe it or not, the mountain had come to Mohammed; their school had come to them. At least, Jamie's class had.

Jamie was furious. Why had Claudia muzzled him? Did she think he had no sense at all? He pulled his eyebrows down and made his best possible scowl. Claudia held her finger up to her lips and signaled

him to stay quiet yet. The sounds of third grade shuffling and third grade jostling faded from their shelter.
The quiet of the ages returned to the tomb.

But not to Jamie. He couldn't contain himself
another minute. He could still feel the pressure of
Claudia's hand over his mouth. "I have half a mind
to join that group and go back with them and just be
mysterious about where I came from."

"If you do that, it'll show that you have half a
mind. Exactly half. Only half. Something I've sus-
pected for a long time. You can't even see that this
is perfect."

"How perfect?"

Claudia slowed down. "You go to the museum
office. Deliver the letter. Tell them you are in the
third grade group that is visiting from Greenwich and
someone asked you to deliver the letter. The teacher
said it would be O.K. If they ask you your name, say
Bruce Lansing. But only if they ask."

"You know, Claude, when I'm not wishing I could
give you a sock right in the nose, I'm glad you're on
my team. You're smart even if you're hard to live
with."

"You'll do it then?" Claudia asked.

"Yeah, I'll do it. It *is* perfect."

"Let's hurry before they come back."

Jamie entered the museum office, and Claudia
stood guard outside the door. She intended to step
inside the office if she spotted the class returning.

Jamie wasn't gone long. Everything had gone well, and they hadn't asked his name. Claudia grabbed his arm as he came out. All the energy of Jamie's wound up nerves let loose. He collapsed as hard as if Claudia had suddenly jumped off the down end of a teeter-totter while he was still sitting on the up end.

"Yikes!" he yelled. Claudia was tempted to muzzle him again, but didn't. Instead she led him out the door into the Fifth Avenue crowd and began walking uptown with him as fast as she could go.

8

On Tuesday they again did their laundry. The product of their efforts this time looked only slightly grayer than it had the time before. Claudia's sweater was considerably shrunken.

They knew that it was too early to get an answer to their letter, but they couldn't resist starting down to Grand Central Post Office to take a look anyway. It was noon by the time they stopped and ate breakfast at a Chock Full O'Nuts on Madison Avenue. They dragged it out beyond the patience of the people who were standing waiting to occupy their seats. Both Claudia and Jamie almost didn't want to look at their box in the post office. As long as they didn't look, they still had hopes that they could find a letter there.

They didn't. They strolled along the streets and

found themselves near the United Nations building. Claudia suggested to Jamie that they take the guided tour she had read about when she was studying the Tourguide Book of the American Automobile Association.

"Today we can learn everything about the U.N."

Jamie's first question was, "How much?"

Claudia challenged him to walk in and find out. Fifty cents. Each. They could go if Claudia was willing to skip dessert that afternoon.

Jamie added, "You know, you can't have your cake and take tours, too."

"How about having tours and hot fudge sundaes, too?" Claudia asked.

They stood in line and got tickets for a tour. The girl selling tickets smiled down at them. "No school today?" she asked casually.

"No," Jamie answered. "The boiler on the furnace broke. No heat. They had to dismiss school. You should have heard the explosion! All the windows rattled. We thought it was an earthquake. Fourteen kids got cuts and abrasions, and their parents are suing the school to pay for their medical expenses. Well, it was about ten in the morning. We had just finished our spelling lesson when . . ."

The man behind Jamie who was dressed in a derby hat and who looked more as if he belonged in the U.N. than visiting it said, "I say, what's holding up this line? *I repeat, what* is *holding* up this line?"

The girl gave Jamie the two tickets. As she did so, the man in the derby hat was already pushing his money onto the counter. The girl looked after Jamie and Claudia as they were leaving and said, "Where is . . ."

She couldn't finish her question. The man in the derby hat was scolding the girl. "No wonder it takes the U.N. forever to get something done. I've never seen a line move more slowly." He only looked as if he belonged; he certainly didn't act it.

The girl blushed as she gave the man his ticket. "I hope you enjoy your tour, sir." She acted as if she belonged.

Jamie and Claudia sat with other ticket holders waiting for their numbers to be called.

Claudia spoke softly to Jamie, "You sure are a fast thinker. Where did you cook up that story about the furnace?"

"I've had it ready and waiting ever since we left home. First chance I've had to use it," he answered.

"I thought I had thought of everything," Claudia said.

"That's O.K."

"You're quite a kid."

"Thanks." Jamie smiled.

The guide who was calling the numbers finally said, "Will the people holding tickets number 106 to 121 please go to the double doors on the wall opposite this desk. There your guide will begin your tour."

Jamie and Claudia went. Their guide was an Indian girl who wore a sari and whose long hair was bound into a single braid that hung down her back to well below her waist. With one hand she lifted the folds of her sari; her walk was flavored by her costume: her steps were short and light and there appeared to be great movement around her knees. Claudia looked at her guide's skin and thought of smoky topaz: November, her mother's birthstone. She listened to her guide's accent and formed the sounds in her mind without listening to what the sounds said.

Thus, when the tour was finished, Claudia was no expert on the United Nations, but she had discovered something: saris are a way of being different. She could do two things, she decided. When she was grown, she could stay the way she was and move to some place like India where no one dressed as she did, or she could dress like someone else—the Indian guide even—and still live in an ordinary place like Greenwich.

"How did you like those ear phones where you can tune in almost any old language at all?" Jamie asked his sister. "Pretty keen, huh?"

Claudia seemed to have a far away look in her eye.

"Yes," she answered. It sounded like "yah-ess." Jamie inspected Claudia closely. She was holding one arm crooked and the other pressed against her stomach. Her steps seemed shorter than usual and lighter than usual, and there appeared to be great movement around her knees.

"What's the matter with you?" he asked. "You got stomach cramps or something?"

Claudia lowered her eyes to him and said, "Jamie, you know, you could go clear around the world and still come home wondering if the tuna fish sandwiches at Chock Full O'Nuts still cost thirty-five cents."

"Is that what gave you stomach cramps?" he asked.

"Oh, just skip it! Just skip it." Claudia knew she would have to discover some other way to be different. Angel *would* help her somehow.

Her hopes centered more than ever on Box 847 in the post office, and the following day when they peeked through its little window, they saw an envelope. Claudia was prepared to be the discoverer of great truths, Greenwich's own heroine of the statue—and only twelve years old. Jamie was so excited that he could hardly get the key into the lock to open the box. Claudia waited while he opened it and the envelope, too. He held the letter unfolded and off-center so that they could read it together. In silence.

Saxonberg, I have here attached a copy of the actual letter which I have in my files:

Dear Friends of the Museum:

We sincerely thank you for your interest in trying to help us solve the mystery of the statue. We have long known of the clue you mention; in fact, that clue remains our strongest one in attributing this work to the master, Michelangelo Buonarroti. Other evidence, however, is necessary, for it is known that Michelangelo did not carve all the marble blocks which were quarried for him and which bore his mark. We cannot ignore the possibility that the work may have been done by someone else, or that someone counterfeited the mark into the stone much later. We summarize the possibilities as follows:

1. The work was designed and done by Michelangelo himself.
2. The work was designed by Michelangelo but done by someone else.
3. The work was neither designed nor done by Michelangelo.

Our hope, of course, is to find evidence to support the first of these three possibilities.

Neither Condivi nor Vasari, Michelangelo's biographers who knew him personally mention the master carving this little angel; they mention only the angel carved for the

*altar in Siena. However, in a letter he wrote
to his father from Rome on August 19, 1497,
Michelangelo mentions ". . . I bought a piece
of marble . . . I keep to myself, and I am
sculpturing an image for my own pleasure."
In the past experts have believed the image
which he sculptured for his own pleasure to
be a cupid. Now, we must examine the possibility that it was an angel.*

*The problem of Angel has now become a
matter for consensus. Four Americans, two
Englishmen, and one German, all of whom
are experts on the techniques of Michelangelo
have thus far examined the statue. We are
presently awaiting the arrival of two more experts from Florence, Italy. After all of these
experts have examined the statue, we will write
a summary of their opinions which we will
release to the press.*

*We greatly appreciate your interest and
would enjoy your disclosing further clues to us
if you find them.*

> *Sincerely,*
>
> *Harold C. Lowery
> Public Relations,
> The Metropolitan Museum of Art*

Claudia and Jamie walked from the post office to

Grand Central Terminal and sat down in the waiting room. They sat perfectly quiet. Disappointed beyond words. Claudia would have felt better if the letter had not been so polite. A nasty letter or a sarcastic one can make you righteously angry, but what can you do about a polite letter of rejection? Nothing, really, except cry. So she did.

Jamie let her cry for a while. He sat there and fidgeted and counted the number of benches. She still cried; he counted the number of people on the benches. She was still at it; he calculated the number of people per bench.

After the big blobs of tears stopped, he said, "At least they treated us like grown-ups. That letter is full of big words and all."

"Big deal," Claudia sobbed. "For all they know, we *are* grown-ups." She was trying to find a corner of her shredded Kleenex that she could use.

Jamie let her sniff some, then he quietly asked, "What do we do now? Go home?"

"What? Go home now? We haven't even got our clothes. And your radio is in the violin case. We'd have to go home absolutely empty handed."

"We could leave our clothes; they're all gray anyway."

"But we never even used your radio. How can we face them at home? Without the radio and all. With nothing." She paused for a minute and repeated, "With nothing. We've accomplished nothing."

"We accomplished having fun," Jamie suggested. "Wasn't that what you wanted when we started out, Claude? I always thought it was."

Claudia began big tears again. "But that was then," she sobbed.

"You said you'd go home after you knew about Angel. Now you know."

"That's it," she sobbed. "I do not know."

"You know that you don't know. Just as the people at the museum don't know. C'mon," he pleaded, "we'll enjoy telling them about how we lived in the museum. The violin case can be evidence. Do you realize that we've lived there a whole week?"

"Yes," Claudia sighed. "Just a week. I feel as if I jumped into a lake to rescue a boy, and what I thought was a boy turned out to be a wet, fat log. Some heroine that makes. All wet for nothing." The tears flowed again.

"You sure are getting wet. You started this adventure just running away. Comfortably. Then the day before yesterday you decided you had to be a hero, too."

"Heroine. And how should I have known that I wanted to be a heroine when I had no idea I wanted to be a heroine? The statue just gave me a chance . . . almost gave me a chance. We need to make more of a discovery."

"So do the people at the museum. What more of

a discovery do you think that you, Claudia Kincaid, girl runaway, can make? A tape recording of Michelangelo saying, 'I did it?' Well, I'll clue you in. They didn't have tape recorders 470 years ago."

"I know that. But if we make a real discovery, I'll know *how* to go back to Greenwich."

"You take the New Haven, silly. Same way as we got here." Jamie was losing patience.

"That's not what I mean. I want to know how to go back to Greenwich different."

Jamie shook his head. "If you want to go different, you can take a subway to 125th Street and then take the train."

"I didn't say *differently*, I said *different*. I want to go back different. I, Claudia Kincaid, want to be different when I go back. Like being a heroine is being different."

"Claudia, I'll tell you one thing you can do different . . ."

"Differently," Claudia interrupted.

"Oh, boloney, Claude. That's exactly it. You can stop ending every single discussion with an argument about grammar."

"I'll try," Claudia said quietly.

Jamie was surprised at her quiet manner, but he continued to be businesslike, "Now about this discovery."

"Jamie, I want to know if Michelangelo did it.

I can't explain why exactly. But I feel that I've got to know. For sure. One way or the other. A real discovery is going to help me."

"If the experts don't know for sure, I don't mind not knowing. Let's get tickets for home." Jamie started toward the New Haven ticket window. Claudia stayed behind. Jamie realized that she was not following, returned to her, and lectured, "You're never satisfied, Claude. If you get all A's, you wonder where are the pluses. You start out just running away, and you end up wanting to know everything. Wanting to be Joan of Arc, Clara Barton, and Florence Nightingown all in one."

"Nightingale," Claudia sighed. She got up then and followed slowly behind her brother. But she was feeling too low to go home. She couldn't. She just couldn't. It just wasn't right.

There were only two windows that didn't say, "*Closed.*" They waited a short while as the man in front of them purchased a red commuter's pass like the one that had brought them to Manhattan.

Jamie addressed the man behind the counter and said, "Two half-fare tickets for . . ."

"FARMINGTON, CONNECTICUT," Claudia broke in.

"To get to Farmington, you have to go to Hartford and take a bus," the ticket agent said.

Jamie nodded to the man and said, "Just a minute,

please." He stepped away from the window, grabbing Claudia's arm. He pulled her away.

Claudia whispered, "Mrs. Basil E. Frankweiler."

"What about Mrs. Basil E. Frankweiler?"

"She lives in Farmington."

"So what?" Jamie said. "The paper said that her house was closed."

"Her New York house was closed. Can't you read anything right?",

"You talk that way, Claude, and . . ."

"All right, Jamie. All right. I shouldn't talk that way. But, please let's go to Farmington. Jamie, please. Can't you see how badly I need to find out about Angel? I just have a hunch she'll see us and that she knows."

"I've never known you to have a hunch before, Claude. You usually plan everything."

"I have, too, had a hunch before."

"When?"

"That night they moved the statue and I stayed in the washroom and didn't get caught. That was a hunch. Even if I didn't know it was a hunch at the time."

"O.K. We'll go to Farmington," Jamie said. He marched to the ticket window and bought passage to Hartford.

They were waiting at track twenty-seven when Claudia said to Jamie, "That's a first for you, too."

"What is?" he asked.

"Buying something without asking the price first."

"Oh, I must have done that before now," he answered.

"When? Name one time."

"I can't think of it right now." He thought a minute then said, "I haven't been a tightwad all my life, have I?"

"As long as I've known you," Claudia answered.

"Well, you've known me for as long as I've known me," he said smiling.

"Yes," Claudia said, "I've been the oldest child since before you were born."

They enjoyed the train ride. A large portion of it went over track they had never before seen. Claudia arrived in Hartford feeling much happier than she had since they received the morning's mail. Her self-assurance had returned to her.

The Hartford station was on Farmington Avenue. Claudia reasoned that they could not be far from Farmington itself. Why take a bus and worry about which stop to get off? Without consulting Jamie she hailed a cab. When it stopped, she got in; Jamie followed. Claudia told the driver to take them to the house of Mrs. Basil E. Frankweiler in Farmington, Connecticut. Claudia sat back. In a taxi at last.

(And that, Saxonberg, is how I enter the story. Claudia and Jamie Kincaid came to see me about Angel.)

9

Up the entire length of my long, wide, tree-lined road they came.

"Do you suppose that Mrs. Frankweiler owns the highway?" Jamie asked.

The taxi driver answered, "This ain't no highway. It's all her propitty. I tell ya, this dame's loaded. In front of the house this here begins to resemble wattcha call a *normal* driveway."

Claudia discovered that indeed it does. My tree-lined avenue circles in front of my house. Jamie looked up at my house and said, "Another museum."

Claudia answered, "Then we should feel very much at home."

Jamie paid the taxi driver. Claudia pulled his arm and whispered, "Tip him."

Jamie shrugged his shoulders and gave the driver some money. The driver smiled, took off his hat, bowed from the waist, and said, "Thank you, sir."

After he drove away Claudia asked, "How much did you give him?"

Jamie answered, "All I had."

"That was stupid," Claudia said. "Now, how are we going to get back?"

Jamie sighed, "I gave him seventeen cents. So it wasn't such a great tip. Also, it would never be enough to get us back. We're broke. How do you feel about that, Miss Taxi Rider?"

"Pretty uncomfortable," she murmured. "There's something nice and safe about having money."

"Well, Claude, we just traded safety for adventure. Come along, Lady Claudia."

"You can't call me Lady Claudia anymore. We're paupers now."

They ascended the low, wide steps of my porch. Jamie rang the bell. Parks, my butler, answered.

"We'd like to see Mrs. Basil E. Frankweiler," Jamie told him.

"Whom shall I say is calling?"

Claudia cleared her throat, "Claudia and James Kincaid."

"Just one moment, please."

They were left standing in the reception hall more than "one-moment-please" before Parks returned.

"Mrs. Frankweiler says she doesn't know you."

"We would like her to," Claudia insisted.

"What is the nature of your business?" he asked. Parks always asks that.

Both hesitated. Jamie decided on an answer first, "Please tell Mrs. Basil E. Frankweiler that we are seeking information about the Italian Renaissance."

Parks was gone a full ten minutes before his second return. "Follow me," he commanded. "Mrs. Frankweiler will see you in her office."

Jamie winked at Claudia. He felt certain that mentioning the Italian Renaissance had intrigued me.

They walked behind Parks through my living room, drawing room, and library. Rooms so filled with antique furniture, Oriental rugs, and heavy chandeliers that you complain that they are also filled with antique air. Well, when a house is as old as mine, you can expect everything in it to be thickened by time. Even the air. My office surprised them after all this. It surprises everyone. (You once told me, Saxonberg that my office looks more like a laboratory than an office. That's why I call what I do there *research*.) I suppose it does look like a lab furnished as it is with steel, Formica, vinyl and lit by fluorescence. You must admit though that there's one feature of the room that looks like an office. That's the rows and rows of filing cabinets that line the walls.

I was sitting at one of the tables wearing my customary white lab coat and my baroque pearl necklace when the children were brought in.

"Claudia and James Kincaid," Parks announced.

I allowed them to wait a good long while. Parks had cleared his throat at least six times before I turned around. (Of course, Saxonberg, you know that I hadn't wasted the time between Park's announcement that Claudia and James Kincaid wanted to see me and the time they appeared at the office. I was busy doing research. That was also when I called you. You sounded like anything but a lawyer when I called. Disgusting!) I could hear the children shuffling back and forth impatiently. The importance of Parks's manner is what kept them from interrupting me. They shuffled and scratched, and Jamie even emitted two very false sneezes to attract my attention. It's particularly easy for me to ignore fake sneezes, and I went on with my research.

I don't like to waste time, so when I at last turned around, I did so abruptly and asked directly, "Are you the children who have been missing from Greenwich for a week?" (You must admit, Saxonberg, that when the need arises, I have a finely developed sense of theatrics.)

They had become so used to not being discovered that they had entirely forgotten that they were runaways. Now their reaction was one of amazement. They both looked as if their hearts had been pushed through funnels.

"All right," I said. "You don't have to tell me. I know the answer."

"How did you know about us?" Jamie asked.

"Did you call the police?" Claudia asked at the same time.

"From the newspapers," I replied, pointing to Jamie. "And no," I replied pointing to Claudia. "Now both of you sit down here and talk about the Italian Renaissance."

Jamie glanced at the newspapers I had been researching. "We're in the newspapers?" He seemed pleased.

"Even your pictures," I nodded.

"I'd like to see that," Claudia said. "I haven't had a decent picture taken since I've been able to walk."

"Here you are." I held out several papers. "Two days before yesterday you were on the fifth page in Hartford, the second page in Stamford and the front page in Greenwich."

"The front page in Greenwich?" Claudia asked.

"That's my school picture from the first grade!" Jamie exclaimed. "See, I don't have one of my front teeth."

"Goodness! This picture of me is three years old. Mother never even bought my school pictures the last two years." Claudia held her picture up for Jamie to see. "Do you think I still look like this?"

"Enough!" I said. "Now, what do you want to tell me about the Italian Renaissance?"

"Is your butler calling the police while you stall us here?" Jamie asked.

"No," I answered. "And I refuse to keep reassuring you. If you keep on with this kind of talk, I shall find you so dull that I shall call your parents as well as the police to get rid of you. Is that clear, young man?"

"Yes," Jamie muttered.

"Young lady?"

Claudia nodded yes. They both stood with bowed heads. Then I asked Jamie, "Do I frighten you, young man?"

Jamie looked up. "No, ma'am. I'm quite used to frightening things. And you're really not so bad looking."

"So bad looking? I wasn't referring to the way I look." Actually, I never think much about that any more. I rang for Parks. When he arrived I told him to please bring me a mirror. Everyone waited in silence until Parks returned with the mirror. Silence continued as I picked it up and began a very long and close inspection of my face.

It's not a bad face except that lately my nose seems to have grown longer, and my upper lip appears to have collapsed against my teeth. These things happen when people get older. And I am getting just that. I ought to do something about my hair besides have Parks cut it for me. It's altogether white now and looks like frayed nylon thread. Maybe, I'll take time out and get a permanent wave, except that I hate beauty parlors.

"My nose has gotten longer. Like Pinocchio. But not for the same reason. Well, not most of the time," I said as I put down the mirror. Claudia gasped, and I laughed. "Oh, so you were thinking the same thing? No matter. I never really look past my eyes. That way I always feel pretty. Windows of the soul, you know."

Claudia took a step closer to me. "You really do have beautiful eyes. They're like looking into a kaleidoscope—the way those golden flecks in them keep catching the light."

She was quite close to me now and actually peering into my face. It was uncomfortable. I put a stop to that.

"Do you spend much time looking in mirrors, Claudia?"

"Some days I do. Some days I don't."

"Would you care to look now?"

"No, thank you," she said.

"Well, then," I said, "we'll continue. Parks, please return this mirror. We want to talk about the Italian Renaissance. James, you haven't said one word since you told me that I look frightening. Speak now."

"We want to know about the statue," Jamie stammered.

"Speak up, boy," I commanded. "What statue?"

"The statue in the Metropolitan Museum in New York City. In Manhattan. The one of the angel."

"The one you sold for $225," Claudia added.

I walked over to my files of newspaper clippings and pulled out a manila folder, the one which has all the newspaper clippings about the auction and the museum buying the statue. It also contains the article about the crowds going to see the statue.

"Why did you sell her?" Claudia asked pointing to the picture of Angel.

"Because I don't like to donate things."

"If I owned such a lovely statue, I'd never sell it. Or donate it either. I'd cherish it like a member of my own family," Claudia preached.

"Considering all the trouble you've caused your family, that isn't saying very much."

"Have they been worried?" she asked.

"If you hadn't been so busy looking at your picture in the paper, you could have read that they are nearly frantic."

Claudia blushed. "But I wrote them a letter. I told them not to worry."

"Evidently your letter didn't work. Everyone is worried."

"I told them not to," she repeated. "We're going home anyway as soon as you tell us if Michelangelo carved Angel. Did he do it?"

"That's my secret," I answered. "Where have you been all week?"

"That's our secret," Claudia answered, lifting her chin high.

"Good for you!" I cheered. Now I was certain that I liked these two children. "Let's go to lunch." Examining the two of them in that bright light I saw that they looked wrinkled, dusty, and gray. I instructed them to wash up while I told the cook to prepare for two more.

Parks led Jamie to one bathroom; my maid, Hortense, led Claudia to another. Apparently, Claudia had never enjoyed washing up so much. She took forever doing it. She spent a great deal of time looking into all the mirrors. Examining her eyes very carefully, she decided that she, too, was beautiful. But mostly her thoughts were about the beautiful black marble bathtub in that bathroom.

(Even in this very elegant house of mine, that bathroom is especially grand. All the walls are black marble except for one that is mirrored entirely. The faucets are gold, and the spigot is shaped like a dragon's head. The tub looks like a black marble swimming pool sunken into the floor; there are two steps down to the bottom.)

There was nothing she wanted more than to take a bath in that tub. She examined her eyes a little longer and then spoke to her image in the mirror, "You'll never have a better chance, Lady Claudia. Go ahead. Do it." So she did. She opened the taps and began undressing as the tub was filling up.

Meanwhile, Jamie had done his customary job of washing up. That is, he had washed the palms but not backs of his hands, his mouth but not the eyes of his face. He emerged from the bathroom long before Claudia and growing impatient, began wandering through rooms until he found Hortense and asked her the whereabouts of his sister. He followed directions to Claudia's bathroom where he heard the water still running. It takes a lot of water to fill that tub.

"Suicide!" he thought. "She's going to drown herself because we're caught." He tried the door; it was locked.

"Claudia," he yelled, "is anything the matter?"

"No," she answered. "I'll be right there."

"What's taking you so long?"

"I'm taking a bath," she called.

"Oh, boloney," Jamie answered. He walked away to find me. I was waiting in the dining room. I'm accustomed to eating on time, and I was hungry.

"That nutty sister of mine is taking a bath. Don't mind her. She even takes baths when she comes in from swimming. She even made us take baths while we were hiding at the Metropolitan Museum. I think we should start without her."

I smiled, "I think, James, that you already have."

I rang for Parks, and he appeared with the salad and began serving.

"How did Claudia manage to take a bath in the museum?" I asked casually.

"In the fountain. It was cold, but I didn't mind when we found . . . Uh oh. Uuuuh. Ooooh. I did it. I told. I did it." He rested his elbow on the table and his chin on his hand. He slowly shook his head "Sometimes I stink at keeping secrets. Don't tell Claudia I told. Please."

"I'm curious to know how you managed." I *was* curious, and you know that I can be absolutely charming when I want information.

"Let Claude tell you all that. She did the planning. I managed the money. She's big on ideas, but she's also big on spending money. I managed fine until today. Now we're broke. Not one cent left to get back to Greenwich."

"You can walk or hitchhike."

"Try telling that to Claude."

"Or you can turn yourselves in. The police will take you back, or your parents will come and get you."

"Maybe that will appeal to Claudia, but I doubt it. Even though she sure doesn't approve of making herself walk."

"Perhaps we can work out a deal. You give me some details, and I'll give you a ride back."

Jamie shook his head. "You'll have to work that out with Claude. The only kind of deal I can make concerns money, and we don't have any more of that."

"You are poor, indeed, if that's the only kind of a deal you can make."

Jamie brightened. "Would you like a game of cards?"

"Which game?" I asked.

"War."

"I assume you cheat."

"Yeah." he sighed.

"I may decide to play after lunch anyway."

"Can we start eating now?" Jamie asked.

"You don't worry about manners too much do you?"

"Oh," he replied, "I don't worry about them too much when I'm this hungry."

"You're honest about some things."

Jamie shrugged his shoulders. "You might say that I'm honest about everything except cards. For some reason I'm helpless about cheating at cards."

"Let's eat," I said. I was anxious, for I do enjoy a good game of cards, and Jamie promised to provide just that.

Claudia appeared as we were finishing our soup. I saw that she was annoyed that we had not waited for her. She was all bound up in concern for good manners, and she wanted very much to let us know that she was annoyed and why. She acted cool. I pretended I didn't notice. Jamie didn't pretend; he simply did not notice.

"I'll skip the soup," Claudia announced.

"It's good," Jamie said. "Sure you don't want to try it?"

"No, thank you," Claudia said. Still cool.

I summoned Parks; he appeared bearing a silver casserole.

"What's that?" Jamie asked.

"*Nouilles et fromage en casserole,*" Parks answered.

Claudia showed interest. "I'll have some, please. Sounds like something special."

Parks served. Claudia looked down at her plate, looked up at me and moaned, "Why, it's nothing but macaroni and cheese."

"You see," I laughed, "under the fancy trappings, I'm just a plain lady."

Claudia laughed then. We all did, and we began enjoying our lunch. I asked Claudia what she would like to do while Jamie and I played cards. She said that she would like to just watch us and think.

"Think about what?"

"About how we're going to get back home."

"Call up your family," I suggested. "They'll come for you."

"Oh, it's so hard to explain over the phone. It will cause so much commotion."

I was astounded. "You still don't think you've caused any commotion so far?"

"I haven't really thought about it very hard. I've been so busy worrying about Michelangelo and avoiding getting caught. If only you'd tell me if the statue was done by Michelangelo. Then I would feel that I could go home again."

"Why would that make a difference?" I asked.

"It would because . . . because . . ."

"Because you found that running away from home didn't make a real difference? You were still the same Greenwich Claudia, planning and washing and keeping things in order?"

"I guess that's right," Claudia said quietly.

"Then why did you run away?"

Claudia's words came slowly; she was forming thoughts into the shape of words for the first time in a long time. "I got the idea because I was mad at my parents. That was getting the idea. Then I started planning it. I thought that I had to think of everything, and I thought of an awful lot. Didn't I, Jamie?" She looked over at her brother, and he nodded. "I enjoyed the planning. Without anyone knowing that I was doing it. I am very good at planning."

"And the more plans you made, the more it became like living at home away from home." I interrupted.

"That's true," she said. "But we did enjoy living away from home in a mild kind of way."

(Notice that Claudia is still being very careful not to reveal to me where she and Jamie stayed. I wasn't ready to push yet. I felt I had to help the child. Don't laugh as you read this, Saxonberg; I do have some charity in me.)

"What part of living away from home did you like the best?"

Jamie answered first, "Not having a schedule."

Claudia became impatient, "But, Jamie, we did have a schedule. Sort of. The best that I could manage under the circumstances. *That* wasn't the most fun part of running away."

"What was the most fun part for you, Claudia?"

"First, it was hiding. Not being discovered. And after hiding became easy, there was Angel. Somehow, Angel became more important than running away."

"How did Angel become involved with your running away?" I purred.

"I won't tell you," Claudia answered.

I put on my surprised look and asked, "Why not?"

"Because if I tell you how Angel got involved, it will be telling you too much else."

"Like telling me where you've been all week?"

"Maybe," she answered coolly.

"Why don't you want to tell me that?"

"I told you before; that's *our* secret."

"Oho! You don't want to lose your bargaining weapon," I crowed. "Is that why you're not telling me where you stayed?"

"That's part of the reason," she said. "The other part is—I think the other part is—that if I tell, then I know for sure that my adventure is over. And I don't want it to be over until I'm sure I've had enough."

"The adventure is over. Everything gets over, and

nothing is ever enough. Except the part you carry
with you. It's the same as going on a vacation. Some
people spend all their time on a vacation taking pictures so that when they get home they can show their
friends evidence that they had a good time. They
don't pause to let the vacation enter inside of them
and take that home."

"Well, I don't really want to tell you where we've
been."

"I know," I answered.

Claudia looked at me. "Do you know I don't want
to tell you, or do you know where we've been? Which
do you mean?"

"Both," I told her quietly. I resumed eating
nouilles et fromage en casserole.

Claudia looked over at Jamie. Jamie had slipped
down in his seat and had thrown his napkin over his
face. Claudia jumped up from her seat, grabbed the
napkin off Jamie's face. Jamie quickly threw his forearms where the napkin had been.

"It slipped, Claude; it slipped out." Jamie's voice
was muted since his forearms were protecting his
mouth.

"Jamie! Jamie! That was all I had. All we had.
The only thing we had left."

"I just forgot, Claude. It's been so long since I've
had a conversation with anyone but you."

"You shouldn't have told her. You heard me say

to her that that was our secret. Twice. Now everything is lost. How can I get her to tell? You had to go and blab it all. Blabbermouth!"

Jamie looked at me for sympathy, "She does get emotional."

"Claudia," I said, "be seated."

She obeyed. I continued. "All is not lost. I'm going to make a bargain with you. Both of you. First of all, stop referring to me as *her*. I am Mrs. Basil E. Frankweiler. Then if you give me all the details of your running away, if you tell me everything—*everything*—I'll give you a ride home. I'll have Sheldon, my chauffeur, drive you home."

Claudia nodded "no."

"A Rolls Royce, Claudia. And a chauffeur. That's a very fine offer," I teased.

Jamie said, "How about it, Claude? It beats walking."

Claudia squinted her eyes and crossed her arms over her chest. "It's not enough. I want to know about Angel."

I was glad that I wasn't dealing with a stupid child. I admired her spirit; but more, I wanted to help her see the value of her adventure. She still saw it as buying her something: appreciation first, information now. Nevertheless, Claudia was tiptoeing into the grown-up world. And I decided to give her a little shove. "Claudia. James. Both of you. Come with me."

We walked single file through several rooms to my office. For a minute I thought I was leader in a game of follow-the-leader.

Jamie caught up with me and said, "For an old lady you sure can walk fast."

Claudia then caught up with Jamie and kicked him.

We arrived at my office, and I motioned for them to sit down.

"Do you see those filing cabinets along that wall?" I asked pointing to the south wall. "Those are my secrets. In one of them is the secret of Michelangelo's Angel. I'll share that secret with you as the rest of my bargain. But now my information is more important than yours. So you must have a handicap. The handicap is that you must find the secret file yourselves, and you have one hour to do it in." I turned to leave, then remembered, "And I don't want my files messed up or placed out of order. They're in a special order that makes sense only to me. If you move things around, I won't be able to find anything. And our whole arrangement will be off."

Jamie spoke, "You sure know how to nervous a guy."

I laughed and left the room. I tiptoed into the large closet I have next to my office. From there I watched and listened to all they did.

Jamie got up immediately and began opening file drawers. Claudia shouted, "STOP!" He did.

"What's the matter with you, Claude? We have only one hour."

"Five minutes of planning are worth fifteen minutes of just looking. Quick, give me the pencil and note pad from that table." Jamie ran to get them. Claudia immediately began making a list. "Here's what we'll look up. I'll take the odd numbers; you take the even."

"I want odd."

"For goodness' sake, Jamie, take odds then."
Here's the list Claudia wrote:

1. Michelangelo
2. Buonarroti
3. Angel
4. Parke Bernet Galleries
5. Metropolitan Museum of Art
6. Italian Renaissance
7. Auctions
8. Sculptor
9. Marble
10. Florence, Italy
11. Rome, Italy

Jamie looked over the list. "I changed my mind. I'll take evens. There's one less."

"Talk about wasting time!" Claudia screamed. "Take evens then, but get to it."

They began to work very rapidly. Claudia once or

twice cautioned Jamie not to make a mess. They had exhausted the list, odds as well as evens. There were folders on most of the categories they looked up, but upon examining them, they found not one hint of Angel. Claudia was feeling depressed. She looked at the clock. Six minutes to go.

"Think, Jamie, think. What else can we look up?"

Jamie squinted his eyes, a sign that he was thinking hard. "Look him up under . . ."

"What kind of language is that? Look him *up under* . . ."

"Oh, boloney, Claude. Why do you always pick on my gra . . ."

"Boloney, boloney! That's it, Jamie. She bought Angel in Bologna, Italy. The paper said so. Look up Bologna." Both ran back to the files and pulled out a file folder fat with papers and documents. It was labeled: BOLOGNA, ITALY. They knew even before opening it that it was the right one. I knew, too. They had found the file that held the secret.

Claudia was no longer in a hurry; she sauntered over to a table, carefully laid down the file, smoothed her skirt under her, and sat in a chair. Jamie was jumping up and down, "Hurry up, Claude. The hour is almost over."

Claudia was not to be hurried. She carefully opened the folder, almost afraid of what she would find. The evidence was sealed between two sheets of glass. The evidence was a very special, very old piece of paper. On one side was written a poem, a sonnet. Since it was written in Italian, neither Claudia nor Jamie could read it. But they could see that the handwriting was angular and beautiful, in itself almost a work of art. And there was a signature: Michelangelo. The other side of the paper needed no translation. For there, in the midst of sketches of hands and torsos was a sketch of someone they knew: Angel. There were the first lines of a thought that was to become a museum mystery 470 years later. There on that piece of old paper was the idea just as it had come from Michelangelo's head to his hand, and he had jotted it down.

Claudia looked at the sketch until its image became blurred. She was crying. At first she said nothing. She simply sat on the chair with tears slowly streaming down her face, hugging the glass frame and shaking her head back and forth. When at last she found her voice, it was a hushed voice, the voice she used for church. "Just think, Jamie, Michelangelo himself touched this. Over four hundred years ago."

Jamie was looking through the rest of the folder. "The glass," he said. "I'll bet he didn't touch the glass. Are his fingerprints on it?" He didn't wait for an answer before asking something else. "What do you suppose the rest of these papers are?"

"They are my research on Angel," I answered as I emerged from my hiding place in the closet. "He did

it in Rome, you know. I just file it under *B* for
Bologna to make it hard."

Both children looked up at me startled. Just as
they had lost all their feelings of urgency, they had
also lost all thoughts of me. Finding a secret can
make everything else unimportant, you know.

Claudia said nothing and nothing and nothing.
She continued clutching the drawing to her chest and
rocking it back and forth. She appeared to be in a
trance. Jamie and I stared at her until she felt our
eyes focused on her like four laser beams. She looked
up at us then and smiled.

"Michelangelo did sculpture the statue, didn't he,
Mrs. Frankweiler?"

"Of course. I've known for a long time that he
did. Ever since I got that sketch."

"How did you get the sketch?" Jamie asked.

"I got it after the war. . . ."

"Which war?" Jamie interrupted.

"World War II. Which war did you think I
meant? The American Revolution?"

"Are you that old?" Jamie asked.

"I'm not even going to answer that."

Claudia said, "Hush, Jamie. Let her tell us." But
she couldn't hush either. She rushed in with an explanation, "I'll bet you helped some rich Italian nobleman or some descendant of Michelangelo's to escape,
and he gave you the sketch out of his undying grati-
tude."

"That's one explanation. But not the correct one. There was a rich Italian nobleman involved. That part is right."

"Did he sell it to you?" Jamie asked.

Claudia rushed in again with another explanation, "He had this beautiful daughter and she needed this operation very badly and you . . ."

Jamie interrupted. "Hush, Claudia." Then he asked me, "Why did he give it to you?"

"Because he was a very, very bad poker player, and I am a very good one."

"You won it at cards?" I could see admiration grow in Jamie's eyes.

"Yes I did."

"Did you cheat?" he asked.

"Jamie, when the stakes are high, I never cheat. I consider myself too important to do that."

Jamie asked, "How come you don't sell the sketch? You could get quite a boodle for it. Being that it matches up with the statue and all."

"I need having the secret more than I need the money," I told him.

I knew that Claudia understood. Jamie looked puzzled.

"Thank you for sharing your secret with us," Claudia whispered.

"How do you know that we'll keep your secret?" Jamie asked.

"Now, now, a boy who cheats at cards should be able to answer that."

Jamie's face broke into a huge grin. "Bribery!" he exclaimed. "You're going to bribe us. Hallelujah! Tell me. I'm ready. What's the deal?"

I laughed. "The deal is this: you give me the details of your running away, and I'll give you the sketch."

Jamie gasped. "That doesn't sound like bribery. That doesn't even sound like you, Mrs. Frankweiler. You're smarter than that. How do you know that I won't slip about your secret as I did about the museum?"

That boy really amused me. "You're right, Jamie. I am smarter than that. I've got a method to keep you slip-proof about the sketch."

"What's that?"

"I'm not going to give you the sketch outright. I'm going to leave it to you in my will. You won't tell my secret because if you do, I'll write you out of my will. You would lose all that money. You said that the sketch was worth quite a boodle. So you're going to be very good about keeping this secret. Claudia will keep quiet for a different reason. Her reason happens to be the same as mine."

"Which is what?" Jamie asked.

"Simply because it is a secret. It will enable her to return to Greenwich *different*."

Claudia looked at Jamie and nodded. Something I had just said made sense.

I continued, "Returning with a secret is what she really wants. Angel had a secret and that made her exciting, important. Claudia doesn't want adventure. She likes baths and feeling comfortable too much for that kind of thing. Secrets are the kind of adventure she needs. Secrets are safe, and they do much to make you different. On the inside where it counts. I won't actually be getting a secret from you; I'll be getting details. I'm a collector of all kinds of things besides art," I said pointing to my files.

"If all those files are secrets, and if secrets make you different on the inside, then your insides, Mrs. Frankweiler, must be the most mixed-up, the most different insides I've ever seen. Or any doctor has ever seen, either."

I grinned. "There's a lifetime of secrets in those files. But there's also just a lot of newspaper clippings. Junk. It's a hodgepodge. Like my art collection. Now, you'll tell me all about your running away, and I'll add that to my files."

Whereas Jamie's excitement bubbled out of him in grins and spurts of jittering around the room, Claudia's excitement flowed not bubbled. I could see that she was a little surprised. She had known that Angel would have the answer, but she had expected it to be a loud bang, not a quiet soaking in. Of course secrets make a difference. That was why planning the runaway had been such fun; it was a secret. And hiding in the museum had been a secret. But they weren't permanent; they had to come to an end. Angel wouldn't. She could carry the secret of Angel inside her for twenty years just as I had. Now she wouldn't have to be a heroine when she returned home . . . except to herself. And now she knew something about secrets that she hadn't known before.

I could tell that she felt happy. Happiness is excitement that has found a settling down place, but there is always a little corner that keeps flapping around. Claudia could have kept her doubts to herself, but she was an honest child, an honorable child.

"Mrs. Frankweiler," she said swallowing hard, "I really love the sketch. I really do. I love it. Just love, love, love it. But don't you think you ought to give it to the museum. They're just dying to find out whether the statue is real or not."

"Nonsense! What a conscience you suddenly have. I want to give it to you. In exchange. If you and Jamie want to give it to the museum after you inherit it, then you give it to the museum. I won't let the museum people near here. If I could keep them out of Connecticut altogether, I would. I don't want them to have it while I'm alive."

Claudia wiped her forehead with the sleeve of her sweater and asked, "Why not?"

"I've thought about that for a long time, and I've decided 'why not?' What they'll do is start investigating the authenticity of the sketch. They'll call in authorities from all over the world. They'll analyze the ink. And the paper. They'll research all his illustrated notes and compare, compare, compare. In short, they'll make a science of it. Some will say 'yes.' Some will say 'no.' Scholars will debate about it. They'll poll all the authorities, and probably the majority will agree that the note and the statue are really the work of Michelangelo. At least that's what they should conclude. But some stubborn ones won't agree, and thereafter the statue and the sketch will appear in books with a big question mark. The experts don't believe in coincidence as much as I do, and I don't want them to throw doubt on something that I've felt always, and actually known for about twenty years."

Claudia's eyes widened, "But, Mrs. Frankweiler, if there is the slightest doubt that either the statue or the sketch is a forgery, don't you want to know? Don't you want the last little bit of doubt cleared up?"

"No," I answered abruptly.

"Why not?"

"Because I'm eighty-two years old. That's why. There now, Jamie, you see, I slip too. Now I've told you how old I am."

Jamie looked at his sister and asked, "What's that got to do with anything, Claude?" Claudia shrugged.

"I'll tell you what it's got to do with it," I said. "I'm satisfied with my own research on the subject. I'm not in the mood to learn anything new."

Claudia said, "But, Mrs. Frankweiler, you should want to learn one new thing every day. We did even at the museum."

"No," I answered, "I don't agree with that. I think you should learn, of course, and some days you must learn a great deal. But you should also have days when you allow what is already in you to swell up inside of you until it touches everything. And you can feel it inside you. If you never take time out to let that happen, then you just accumulate facts, and they begin to rattle around inside of you. You can make noise with them, but never really feel anything with them. It's hollow."

Both children were quiet, and I continued. "I've gathered a lot of facts about Michelangelo and Angel. And I've let them grow inside me for a long time. Now I feel that I know. That's enough for that. But there is one new thing that I'd like to experience. Not know. Experience. And that one thing is impossible."

"Nothing is impossible," Claudia said. She sounded to me exactly like a bad actress in a bad play—unreal.

"Claudia," I said patiently, "When one is eighty-two years old, one doesn't have to learn one new thing every day, and one knows that some things are impossible."

"What would you like to experience that is impossible?" Jamie asked.

"Right now, I'd like to know how your mother feels."

"You keep saying that she's frantic. Why do you want to feel frantic?" This came from Claudia. Now she sounded like the real Claudia Kincaid.

"It's an experience I would like to have because it's part of a bigger experience I want."

Claudia said, "You mean you'd like to be a mother?"

Jamie leaned toward Claudia and whispered in the loudest, wettest whisper I have ever heard, "Of course that's impossible. Her husband is dead. You can't be a mother without a husband."

Claudia poked Jamie, "Never call people *dead*; it makes others feel bad. Say 'deceased' or 'passed away.'"

"Come now, children. Put away the file. You must tell me all about your adventure. All, all, all about it. What you thought and what you said and how you managed to carry off the whole crazy caper."

10

I KEPT THE CHILDREN UP LATE GETTING THE DETAILS.
Jamie and I played war while Claudia talked into the
tape recorder. Jamie ended up with two aces and
twelve cards more than I; the game cost me thirty-four
cents. I still don't know how he does it. It was my
deck of cards; but I was somewhat preoccupied listening to Claudia and interrupting her with questions.
And then there was that telephone call from the children's parents. I knew you'd tell them, Saxonberg.
I knew it! What a combination you are: soft heart
and hard head. It was all I could do to persuade them
to stay home and let me deliver the children in the
morning. Mrs. Kincaid kept asking if they were
bruised or maimed. I think she has read too many

accounts of lost children in the newspapers. You realize now why I insisted that they stay overnight. I
wanted all sides of the bargain kept, and I had to get
my information. Besides I had promised them a ride
home in the Rolls Royce, and I never cheat when the
stakes are high.

When it came to be Jamie's turn to talk into the
tape recorder, I thought that I would never get him
to quit fussing with the switches. He enjoyed saying
something and then erasing it. Finally, I scolded him,
"You're not Sir Lawrence Olivier playing Hamlet,
you know. All I want are the facts and how you felt.
Not a theatrical production."

"You want me to be accurate, don't you?"

"Yes, but I also want you to finish."

Claudia asked for a tour of the house while Jamie
told his story. She asked about everything. We rode
the elevator up to the third floor, and she went from
one room to the next. I hadn't been through the entire house for a long time, so I enjoyed the tour, too.
We talked; we both enjoyed that also. Claudia told
me about her routine at home. When we came back
to the black marble bathroom, she told me how she
came to take a bath there earlier. I allowed her to pick
the bedroom where she would sleep that night.

Very early the next morning I had Sheldon drive
them to Greenwich. I'm enclosing a copy of his report
for your amusement, Saxonberg; you ought to be in
a mood to laugh now.

The boy, madam, spent the first five minutes of the trip pushing every button in the back seat. I transported them in the Rolls Royce as you requested. He pushed some buttons at least twelve times; others I stopped counting at five. He seemed to regard the button panel, madam, as some sort of typewriter or piano or I.B.M. computer. Without realizing it he pushed the button to the intercom *on* and neglected to push it *off*. In this way I overheard all their conversation; they thought they were privately sealed behind the glass screen that divides the front seat from the back. The girl was quiet while the other tested things. Everything, I might add.

Finally, the girl remarked to the other, "Why do you suppose she sold Angel in the first place? Why didn't she just donate it to the museum?"

"Because she's tight. That's why. She said so," the boy answered.

"That's not the reason. If she were tight, and she knew it was worth so much, she would never have sold it for $225."

Thank goodness the girl interested him in conversation. He stopped pushing buttons. Besides neglecting to turn off the intercom, he also neglected to turn off the windshield wipers on the rear window. I might add, madam, that it was not raining.

"Well, she sold it at auction, silly. At an auction you have to sell it to the highest bidder. No one bid higher than $225. It's that simple."

The girl replied, "She didn't sell it for the money. She would have shown her evidence if she really wanted a big price. She sold it for the fun of it. For excitement."

"Maybe she didn't have room for it anymore."

"In that museum of a house? There're rooms upstairs that . . . oh! Jamie, the statue is only two feet tall. She could have tucked it into any corner."

"Why do *you* think she sold it?"

The girl thought a minute. (I was hoping she would answer soon, madam. Before the boy got interested in the buttons again.) "Because after a time having a secret and nobody knowing you have a secret is no fun. And although you don't want others to know what the secret is, you want them to at least know you have one."

I observed from the rear view mirror, madam, that the little boy grew quiet. He looked at the girl and said, "You know, Claude, I'm going to save my money and my winnings, and I'm going to visit Mrs. Frankweiler again." A long pause, then, "There's something about our running away that I forgot to say into the tape recorder."

The girl said nothing.

"Wanna come, Claude? We won't tell anyone."

"How much did you win last night?" the girl asked.

"Only thirty-four cents. She's a lot sharper than Bruce."

"Maybe my twenty-five cents from the corn-flakes came already. That would make fifty-nine." The girl was silent for a few minutes before she asked, "Do you think she meant that stuff about motherhood?"

The boy shrugged his shoulders. "Let's visit her every time we save enough money. We won't tell anyone. We won't stay overnight. We'll just tell Mom and Dad that we're going bowling or something, and we'll take a train up instead."

"We'll adopt her," the girl suggested. "We'll become her kids, sort of."

"She's too old to be a mother. She said so herself. Besides, we already have one."

"She'll become our grandmother, then, since ours are deceased."

"And that will be our secret that we won't even share with her. She'll be the only woman in the world to become a grandmother with never becoming a mother first."

I drove the car to the address they gave me, madam. The shades were up, and I could see a quite handsome man and a young matron watching by the window. I also thought I saw our own Mr. Saxonberg. The boy had opened the doors even before I had completely stopped. That is a very dangerous thing to do. A much younger creature, also a boy, came running out of the house immediately ahead of the others. As I drove away, this younger one was saying, "Boy! what a car. Hey, Claude, I'll be your *sponsibility* the rest of . . ."

The children, madam, neglected to say thank you.

Well, Saxonberg, that's why I'm leaving the drawing of Angel to Claudia and Jamie Kincaid, your two lost grandchildren that you were so worried about. Since they intend to make me their grandmother, and you already are their grandfather, that makes us—oh, well, I won't even think about that. You're not that good a poker player.

Rewrite my will with a clause about my bequeath-
ing the drawing to them. Also put in a clause about
that bed I mentioned, too. I guess I ought to donate
it to the Metropolitan Museum. I haven't really begun to like donating things. You'll notice that everyone is getting these things after I'm dead. I should
say *passed away*. After you have all those things written into my will, I'll sign the new version. Sheldon
and Parks can be witnesses. The signing of the will
will take place in the restaurant of the Metropolitan
Museum of Art in New York City. You'll come there
with me, dear Saxonberg, or lose me, your best client.

I wonder if Claudia and Jamie will come visit me
again. I wouldn't mind if they did. You see, I still
have an edge; I know one bit more of a secret than
they do. They don't know that their grandfather has
been my lawyer for forty-one years. (And I recom-
mend that for your own good, you not tell them,
Saxonberg.)

By the way I heard a radio interview by the new
Commissioner of Parks in New York City. He said
that his budget had been cut. When asked by a re-
porter where the money that should have been spent
for the parks was going, the commissioner replied that
most of it was going towards increased security for the
Metropolitan Museum. Suspecting that something
special had prompted this move, I asked Sheldon to
call his friend, Morris the guard, to find out if any-

thing unusual had been discovered lately.

Morris reported that a violin case was found in a sarcophagus last week. A trumpet case was found two days later. Morris says that guards who have worked at the museum for a year have seen everything; those who have worked there for six months have seen half of everything. They once discovered a set of false teeth on the seat of an Etruscan chariot. They sent the children's cases to Lost and Found. They are still there. Full of gray-washed underwear and a cheap transistor radio. No one has claimed them yet.